"I'm worend to **be here for you until I know there's no more danger to you."**

Jake took another step closer, now invading her personal space and bringing with him his familiar scent. "It's just been notes left in the mailbox and nothing more dangerous than that," Eva replied.

"But we can't know what might happen next and that's what has me worried for you." His gaze bore into hers and for a moment she couldn't breathe. "Right now it's just notes."

He looked at her now the same way he had then... when she'd been sixteen years old and they had been madly in love. His dark, sinful eyes beckoned her forward, to take the last small step between them and fall into his arms.

For just a brief moment she wanted to fall. She wanted to be in his strong arms and feel his lips on hers. She remembered the magic, the all-consuming passion they had once shared, and there was a part of her that wanted to feel that again.

STALKED IN THE NIGHT

New York Times **Bestselling Author**

CARLA CASSIDY

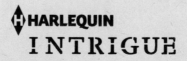

HARLEQUIN®
INTRIGUE®

Recycling programs for this product may not exist in your area.

ISBN-13: 978-1-335-13680-0

Stalked in the Night

Copyright © 2020 by Carla Bracale

This edition published by arrangement with Harlequin Books S.A.

For questions and comments about the quality of this book, please contact us at CustomerService@Harlequin.com.

Harlequin Enterprises ULC
22 Adelaide St. West, 40th Floor
Toronto, Ontario M5H 4E3, Canada
www.Harlequin.com

Printed in U.S.A.

Carla Cassidy is an award-winning, *New York Times* bestselling author who has written over 150 novels for Harlequin. In 1995, she won Best Silhouette Romance from *RT Book Reviews* for *Anything for Danny*. In 1998, she won a Career Achievement Award for Best Innovative Series from *RT Book Reviews*. Carla believes the only thing better than curling up with a good book to read is sitting down at the computer with a good story to write.

Books by Carla Cassidy

Harlequin Intrigue

Desperate Strangers
Desperate Intentions
Desperate Measures
Stalked in the Night

Scene of the Crime

Scene of the Crime: Bridgewater, Texas
Scene of the Crime: Bachelor Moon
Scene of the Crime: Widow Creek
Scene of the Crime: Mystic Lake
Scene of the Crime: Black Creek
Scene of the Crime: Deadman's Bluff
Scene of the Crime: Return to Bachelor Moon
Scene of the Crime: Return to Mystic Lake
Scene of the Crime: Baton Rouge
Scene of the Crime: Killer Cove
Scene of the Crime: Who Killed Shelly Sinclair?
Scene of the Crime: Means and Motive

Visit the Author Profile page at Harlequin.com.

CAST OF CHARACTERS

Eva Martin—Single mother who lives on her ranch. Recently she's received death threats, and when those threats take a turn for the worse, she's terrified and has no idea who wants her dead.

Jake Albright—He has returned to his hometown of Dusty Gulch for two reasons: to bury his father and to see Eva Martin, the woman who broke his heart ten years ago.

Jimmy Miller—Eva's ranch hand. Does he want more from Eva than she's willing to give?

Griff Ainsley—Is the teenager looking for revenge on Eva because she stopped him and his friends from partying in her barn?

Robert Stephenson—Has he tired of Eva's rejections of him and now has a burning hatred for the beautiful woman?

Ben Wilkins—Eva fired the man as a ranch hand. Is he now making her pay?

Chapter One

Eva Martin used the tip of a shovel to poke at the mutilated dead cow on the ground before her, and then she turned and stared up at the tall, uniformed man standing next to her.

Sheriff Wayne Black took off his hat and wiped his sweating face and head with a handkerchief. The month of August in Dusty Gulch, Kansas, could be sweltering, and even though it was only midmorning, the temperature had already reached into the nineties.

Eva had a burn in her chest that had nothing to do with the heat of the day. It was the slow burn of anger, coupled with more than a whisper of fear.

"Wayne, this is the third mutilated cow I've had in as many weeks, and I'm sure if I check my mailbox right now, there'll be another threatening note for me inside."

Wayne swiped the sides of his face once again and then plopped his hat back on his head and gazed out into the distance. "Well, then I guess we'd better check out your mailbox."

As he got back into his patrol car, Eva placed the shovel on the ground next to the dead cow and then mounted her horse, Thunder, and galloped ahead toward the mailbox at the end of the lane to her house.

Her heart beat in her ears almost as loudly as Thunder's hooves against the hard ground. Somebody was targeting her, and she had no idea who it might be. And what frustrated her as much as anything was that she didn't believe the sheriff was taking any of this seriously enough.

In a town practically owned by the powerful Albright family, she knew Wayne saw her as nothing more than a pesky gnat to be swatted away. Wayne Black was Justin Albright's man, and she was definitely not a fan of the Albrights. She'd never pretended to be.

She got to the mailbox first and then waited for Wayne to pull up and get out of his patrol car. She opened the mailbox, and just as she'd suspected, there was a plain white envelope addressed to her in bold black block lettering.

Even though she had received two notes before, her heartbeat accelerated and her chest tightened as she grabbed the envelope from the mailbox. She opened it and fought off a small shiver as she read, "Whore—get out of town."

"That's pretty much like the last two," Wayne said. She held the note out to him, but he didn't take it from her. "I don't need it. I've got the other ones to work with."

"So, what are you doing about this?" Eva asked. "Wayne, you should know I can't afford to lose a cow a week, and these notes definitely seem like a threat to me."

"I know, and I'm investigating it. I promise I'll call you once I have any information to give you."

To her dismay, but not her surprise, he immediately got back into his patrol car and waved to her as he drove away. "He'll call me—yeah, right," she said to her horse.

It had been two weeks since she'd found her first dead cow in her pasture. The cow's throat had been slashed and the heart had been cut out. That day she had also received the first note.

Wayne had come out both previous times and had promised both an investigation and a phone call to tell her what the investigation had found. So far there had been no follow-up phone calls, and she had a sneaking suspicion there had not been much of an investigation.

If she was part of the Albright family or was one of the people in town who kissed Justin Albright's ring, she was certain Wayne would be turning himself inside out to solve these crimes.

She remounted Thunder and headed toward the barn in the distance. She hated to call Harley, one of her ranch hands, and tell him he had to dispose of yet another dead animal.

Still, despite the discovery of another dead cow, as she rode back she couldn't help but feel a small sense of pride. Although a bit skittish, the rest of the herd was all healthy, and when the time came, the sale of them should refill her bank account—which was running dangerously low.

The large garden by the house was still yielding plenty of fresh vegetables, and her chickens were laying enough eggs that she was selling them to the locals.

Her father would have been proud of her and all her hard work to stay on the land he had loved, the land he had worked on all his life. Eva's mother had died when she was eight years old. It had just been her and her father after that. They had been both partners and best friends.

It was difficult for her to believe that he'd been gone for almost ten years. He'd died of a heart attack out in the pasture while he and Eva had been putting out hay for the cattle.

And then there had been Andrew. Her heart squeezed tight as memories of her husband flashed through her head. Andrew had been one of the kindest, most gentle men she'd ever known, and not a day went by that she didn't think of him and miss him.

Once she got back to the house, she made the call to Harley and then headed for a quick shower. Even though it was only midmorning, she felt grimy and like the odor of the cow's death clung to her.

She finished showering and pulled on a summer

shift in shades of blue and violet and then went into the kitchen and made herself a cup of coffee.

She sank down at the kitchen table and drew in a deep breath. Aside from being ticked off by a sheriff she didn't believe was taking the dead cattle and the notes all that seriously, for the first time since her father had died, she was truly afraid.

Who was behind the mutilated cattle and the threatening notes? The whole thing was so sick. Why the taking of the cows' hearts? Was it part of some sort of ritual practiced by some group of nuts in this area? Was it the work of a single person? Why was she the target of such madness?

Her gaze landed on a picture hanging on the far wall. The young boy in the photo was so handsome, with his mop of dark hair and a bright smile that warmed everyone around him.

Her heart squeezed even tighter. She had to stay strong for nine-year-old Andy. Her son was what kept her going, the boy who filled her life with such sunshine and love.

The last thing she wanted was for him to see her fear. She didn't want him to know about the notes or the dead cows. Andy was an innocent child, and she didn't want him to have to deal with any adult issues. He'd already had to deal with far too many.

Three short knocks on her back door announced Harley's arrival. "Come in," she yelled.

Harley Graham had worked as a ranch hand for her for the past seven years. He was older and seasoned and had become both a good friend and mentor. He stepped into the kitchen, and she motioned him toward the coffee maker.

Neither of them spoke until he'd poured his coffee and then joined her at the table. He swept his brown cowboy hat off his head, exposing shaggy gray hair, and set it down in the empty chair next to him.

He gazed at her for a long moment and then shook his head ruefully as deep frown lines cut across his weathered forehead. "Bad business going on here," he said. "Was it the same as last time?"

She nodded. "The heart was cut out."

"And did you get another one of those notes?"

She motioned to the piece of paper folded up next to her on the table. "Same kind of thing...leave town...blah, blah."

Harley's frown deepened. "You called the sheriff?"

She nodded. "He came out."

"And what did he have to say?" Harley took a drink of his coffee.

"The same thing he said the last two times...he's investigating and he'll be in touch."

Harley snorted. "That man isn't capable of investigating his way out of a paper bag. The only reason he's sheriff out here is because he's Albright's yesman. And speaking of the Albrights, did you hear the latest news?"

"What news?" she asked curiously.

"Rumor is old man Albright died sometime early yesterday evening."

Eva stared at him in stunned surprise. Justin Albright was gone? The powerful monster who had forever changed the course of her life had died?

She didn't even know how to feel about it. A curious numbness overtook her. She'd never prayed for the old man's death, but if she was honest with herself, she certainly felt no grief at his passing.

"I wonder how much will change around here with him gone," she finally managed to say.

"I've heard his son David is a fairly decent man. Don't know much about the older son, since the whole time I've been here in Dusty Gulch he's apparently been off someplace in Europe."

"Italy. He's been in Italy running the family's wine business," she replied. Despite the heat of the day, she wrapped her fingers around her cup, seeking warmth for her fingers that had suddenly turned cold.

"What's his name… Jack?"

"Jake," she replied. Even saying his name aloud twisted a ribbon of apprehension and a million other emotions in the pit of her stomach.

"I suppose he'll be flying in for a funeral. Wonder if, as the eldest son, he'll decide to stay on here in town." Harley took another big drink of his coffee and then stood. "Oh well, Albright business is none of my business. I'll just head out of here and take care of that dead cow." He placed his cup in the sink.

"Thanks, Harley. I really appreciate it."

"I'll check in with you later." With a slam of the back door, he was gone.

Eva took a drink of her cooling coffee and tried to keep her thoughts away from Jake Albright. However, it was impossible. Memories of him now blew through her brain like a hot wind that whispered of a wild desire and a certain kind of madness.

It had been the madness of youth and first love, and a depth of passion and desire she'd thought she couldn't live without…until it had all been stolen away.

Over the years she had occasionally seen pictures of him in the society pages of their weekly newspaper. *Jake Albright, wine mogul, shares his birthday or whatever with an Italian model or popular actress or heir to a fortune.* The women had all looked beautiful and polished in a way only money could buy.

She finished her coffee and jerked herself out of the chair and to the sink. She refused to waste another minute of thought on Jake. Just as she was certain he'd never wasted more than a minute of thought about her when he'd left her and Dusty Gulch far behind.

Besides, she was perfectly satisfied alone on her ranch with her son. Andy was all that was important to her, and she didn't need or want any part of Jake or any other man in her life. Hopefully he would fly in for his father's funeral and then be on the next plane back to Italy and she'd never have to see or speak to him again.

JAKE WALKED THROUGH the front door of the mansion where he'd been born, although he certainly felt no sense of homecoming. This big house had never held the warmth of a real home. He'd been raised by a parade of nannies and an autocratic and cold father, and now that man was gone forever.

Justin Albright had been a stern, distant father, but Jake had loved his father deeply and mourned his passing. Now there was no more time for him to get closer with his father, who had died of a sudden, massive heart attack.

He set his suitcase down just inside the front door and went in search of his brother. He found David with his wife, Stephanie, and their five-year-old son, Richard, eating lunch at the table in the elegant dining room.

"Hey, man!" David exclaimed at the sight of Jake, and both he and Stephanie rose from the table. David pulled him into a quick hug and then released him. "Why didn't you call us to let us know when you were getting in? We could have picked you up from the airport."

The Dusty Gulch airport was little more than a single runway used mostly by crop dusters and small planes. There was no outbuilding except a huge shed where some of the locals kept their planes.

"I caught a ride with Lionel," Jake replied. Lionel Watkins was the pilot of the private jet the Albright family used. "Sit down and finish your meal."

"Have you eaten?" Stephanie asked. "I can get Cookie to bring in another plate."

"Thanks. That would be great." Jake sat next to his nephew as Stephanie disappeared into the kitchen. "How are you doing, big guy?" he said to Richard. The dark-haired boy smiled and ducked his head shyly.

Stephanie came back to the table, and a moment later Cookie came into the room with a plate and silverware for Jake. She laid it down before him and then he rose and gathered the chubby woman into his arms for a loving hug.

Carol Simon, aka Cookie, had not only been the Albright cook for thirty years, she had also been a surrogate mother to Jake since his mother had died when he'd been six.

During his childhood there had been many mornings when he'd sneaked into the kitchen and sat at the counter to eat a piece of cinnamon toast while Cookie prepared breakfast for the family. They would talk about anything and everything, and she'd been a warm and loving presence in his life.

"I've missed you, Cookie," he said as he released her.

"Ah, go on with yourself." Her smile moved her plump cheeks upward into a warm smile. "Now, sit and eat. You look like you need some fattening up with some of my good food—stick-to-your-ribs cooking instead of all that foreign junk you've been living on."

Jake laughed and resumed his seat at the table.

Despite the levity of the moment, the conversation quickly turned more somber as they discussed the plans for their father's funeral in three days.

"Dad already arranged everything in the event of his death," David said. "We have an appointment with Paul tomorrow at noon for the reading of the will and then at four we're to meet with Aaron at the funeral home to make sure everything is ready for the funeral at ten on Sunday morning."

Jake nodded. "I'll be available for whatever."

"I had the staff ready your suite for you. How long do you intend to stay?" Stephanie asked.

"I'm here to stay for good," Jake replied. He saw the surprise not only on Stephanie's face but on his brother's as well. "I've been planning on making the move back here for some time. The winery is running smoothly with the managers that are in place. I'm no longer needed there for the day-to-day running of anything, and I've been homesick."

"So, what are your plans?" David asked.

Jake laughed. "I've only been here for less than an hour. To be honest, the only plan I have right now is to freshen up a bit and then head into town and take a look around."

"You'll see a lot of changes have occurred in the past ten years," David said. "We have a new bakery and ice cream parlor on Main and a lot of other businesses that have opened up."

"We even have a ladies' shoe shop," Stephanie said.

Jake smiled teasingly at his sister-in-law. He'd always liked Stephanie. She had gone to high school with Jake and David, but they hadn't started dating until several years later. With her light blond hair and steel blue eyes, she appeared cold and haughty, but nothing could be further from the truth. She was a sweet person with a good and giving heart. "A women's shoe store... wow, Dusty Gulch has definitely arrived," Jake teased.

They all laughed and finished with lunch. Minutes afterward, Jake climbed the main staircase to his suite of rooms in the left wing of the house.

He'd grown up in the suite that included a living area with a fireplace, the bedroom and bathroom. The walls were a pale gray and the furniture was black. There were two leather chairs facing the fireplace and a small sofa against one wall.

He went into the bedroom, where a spread of various shades of gray covered the king-size bed. It had been here in this room where he'd dreamed and planned his future, and it had been in here he'd wept when those dreams had all fallen apart.

His suitcases were already there and awaited his unpacking. He took a quick shower and shaved and then pulled on a pair of jeans and a black polo shirt. He then headed back down the stairs.

David had disappeared into their father's office, and Stephanie was in the kitchen lingering over a cup of coffee. Jake grabbed his truck keys off the key holder where they'd always been held in the kitchen.

"David had your truck serviced this morning, so it would be ready for you," she said.

"That was thoughtful of him," Jake replied. "I appreciate him taking care of my baby while I was gone." His "baby" was the black pickup truck with all the bells and whistles he'd received ten years ago from his father upon his graduation from high school. He'd barely had a chance to enjoy it before he'd left for Italy.

More than that, the truck had been a promise from his father that he would eventually run the ranching portion of the Albright estate, something he'd dreamed of doing since he'd been a young boy.

But that had been before his life had fallen apart. That had been before *her*. Even though it had been ten years since he'd seen her, been with her, thoughts of her still shot a hot wave through his body. He was never sure whether it was the burn of a rich anger he'd never gotten over or the white-hot fever of a desire that had never burned itself out.

"Should I expect you back here for dinner?" Stephanie asked, pulling him from his wayward thoughts.

"No, I'll just grab something while I'm out, but tell David I'll be ready for the appointment at the lawyer's office at noon tomorrow."

"I'll tell him," she replied. "And enjoy your first day home."

"Thanks, Steph. I'll see you later."

Jake stepped out the back door and drew in a deep breath of the August heat. It smelled of pasture and hay and cattle. It was a welcome scent. He'd never wanted to be in Italy working for the family winery. His heart had always been here in Dusty Gulch. But, when his father had insisted he go, Jake had believed there was nothing left here for him, and all he'd wanted to do was escape.

Times had changed. Justin Albright was dead, and Jake's grief was deep for the man he'd admired and loved and desperately wanted to please. His grief came from the fact that he would now never gain the closeness he'd wanted with his father. He'd always thought there would be time for him and his father, but time had run out.

He headed toward the garage in the distance. Once there he got into his pickup and headed out. He followed the drive around to the front of the house, where he had a view of the small town below...a town nearly owned by the Albright family.

He had no idea how his father might have divided things up between him and his brother. Hopefully David would be agreeable to letting Jake take over the ranching business and David would be kept busy with the real estate and any other business.

When he reached the bottom of the hill, instead of turning left to head into town, he turned right and headed in the direction of Eva's place.

He knew going to see Eva Taylor, now Eva Martin, was a foolish thing to do. He'd been seventeen years old and she'd been sixteen when they'd first begun dating. Eventually they had shared an explosive love affair. She'd been his first lover and he had been hers. That had been over ten years ago.

In those ten years, she'd married and had a child and was now a widow. He had no idea why he wanted to see her again, but as he drew closer to her small ranch on the outskirts of town, the nerves in his chest bunched and tightened.

He didn't know why he suddenly felt so tense. She'd really been nothing more to him than a first love…a high school sweetheart. Maybe he just needed to see her again in order to stamp closure on the fiery relationship that had haunted him over the years.

As he pulled down the long lane that was her driveway, he saw the ranch house looked much the way he remembered it. Painted white with dark green shutters and trim, this place had been where he had spent much of his teenage years.

Spending time here with Eva and her father, Tom, had felt like home. Tom had welcomed him like a son, and there had been much warmth and laughter and caring in this small ranch house.

He pulled up and parked, and his gaze swept the area. Although the house appeared to be in good shape, her barn and some of the other outbuildings were weatherworn and begged for paint and some repairs.

Was she struggling financially? It must be hard for a single woman with a son to keep a ranch up and running. He knew they had struggled with money issues when her father had been alive. *None of your business*, a small voice whispered in his head.

He got out of his truck but stood hesitantly by the driver's door. What in the hell was he doing? He shouldn't have come here.

Ten years ago she'd broken up with him, and she had never indicated that she'd regretted her decision. She'd moved on with her life and had probably never given him a second thought.

He was just about to return to his truck and drive away when the front door opened and there she stood.

Clad in a sleeveless summer dress and with her long black hair falling down beyond her shoulders, her beauty nearly stole his breath away.

Her violet-blue eyes were widened in surprise. "Jake," she murmured. "Wha…what are you doing here?"

"I just thought I'd stop by and visit an old friend," he replied. He gestured toward the door. "Can I come in? Maybe get a cup of coffee?"

She hesitated for a long moment, and once again he wondered what in the hell he was doing here. She was even more beautiful than she had been ten years ago, but she definitely didn't appear overjoyed to see him again. And why should she? He was probably nothing more than a distant memory in her mind.

She'd married her husband months after Jake had left town. She'd had his child. Jake had been nothing more to her than a high school boyfriend. But high school had been over a long time ago.

She finally opened the door wider to allow him entry. As he swept by her, he couldn't help but notice the scent that wafted from her. It was the same perfume she'd worn years ago, a spicy, slightly floral scent that instantly heated his blood.

And that's when he knew exactly why he was here. He wanted her. He'd never stopped wanting her. And he believed the only way he could really move on from her was to have her one more time.

Chapter Two

Eva led Jake through the living room and into her kitchen, where he sat at the square wooden table. She went to her coffee maker to start a pot.

She felt as if she was in some kind of shock. Suddenly her body felt too warm, and yet her brain was frozen. The last person on earth she'd expected to see here was Jake Albright, and the surprise of him being here had definitely thrown her for a loop.

As she measured the coffee, she was acutely aware of his gaze on her. What was he doing here? Why had he come? What did he want from her? It felt so surreal to have him in her home…at her table after all these years.

Thank God Andy was still at school. There was no way she wanted her son to have anything to do with Jake Albright. As far as she was concerned, the Albrights' wealth and power-wielding ways had always tainted everything around them.

As the coffee began to drip into the carafe, she finally turned to face him. "What are you doing here, Jake?" She remained standing at the counter.

"I got into town earlier, and I thought about you and decided to stop by and catch up with you." He smiled at her, a slow, sexy rise of his sensual lips that had once weakened her knees. She steeled herself against any emotional response to him.

He had a strong jawline and sculpted features that still made him the most handsome man she had ever known. For a moment there was a long, awkward pause between them.

"I was sorry to hear about your father's death," she finally said, breaking the uncomfortable silence.

A sharp grief splashed over his handsome face. It was there for only a moment and then gone. "Thanks, and I was sorry to hear about your father and your husband. That's a lot of loss for one person to deal with."

"I got through it." She turned around and poured them each a cup of coffee and then joined him at the table. She sat close enough that she could smell him...the scent of clean male with a hint of shaving cream and a fresh-scented cologne.

She still didn't know why he was here. The last time they'd seen each other, they certainly hadn't parted as friends. Rather it had been an emotional time that had ended in acrimony on his part.

"So, how long are you in town for?" she asked and cast her gaze just slightly over his head.

The last thing she wanted to do was gaze into his eyes. Jake's eyes had always been seductive. Dark as night and with long, thick black lashes, there had been a time when she'd easily fallen into the sweet seduction they offered.

Not now.

Not ever again.

"I've been homesick for quite some time, so now I'm in town to stay," he said.

"Oh," she replied, both surprised and dismayed by his response. She'd hoped he'd be on a plane back to Italy as soon as his father was buried. Life had been easier on her without Jake Albright being in town. She certainly didn't want to be reminded of her past mistakes and the secret she needed to keep from him forever.

He leaned back in the chair. He was a tall man with lean lines, but muscled biceps bulged out from beneath his short shirtsleeves, biceps that spoke of an understated strength.

Even as a teenager Jake had possessed a presence that demanded respect. He'd been a leader, never a follower, and he'd had a self-confidence even then that had been appealing. It was as if he owned the air around him. She realized he had that same kind of presence still.

"So, tell me how things have been going around here. The house looks just like I remember it."

"I've managed to keep it up okay, but the barn needs some major repairs. I'm hoping to get on that as soon as possible," she replied.

His gaze landed on the picture of Andy hanging on the wall. "Is that your son?"

Her stomach muscles tightened, and her throat closed up. "Yes, that's Andy," she finally managed to say. She was grateful her voice sounded perfectly normal.

"He's a good-looking boy. He looks a lot like you," he replied and then, to her relief, he looked out the nearby window. "Business is good?"

"We're getting by," she replied and then frowned. The note she had received that morning was still in the middle of the table, and as she stared at it, a faint chill once again filled her body.

She released a deep sigh. "But somebody is not too happy with me right now."

"What does that mean?" One of his dark eyebrows rose slightly.

"Every week for the last three weeks, I've found one of my cows dead and mutilated in the pasture."

His eyes narrowed, and he sat up straighter in the chair. "What do you mean? Mutilated how?"

"Their throats were slashed and then the hearts were removed."

He stared at her. "What the hell?"

She reached out and picked up the note that had arrived that day and tossed it to him. "And each time I've found a dead cow, I've also received one of these in my mailbox."

She watched closely as he read the note. She wasn't sure why she'd told him about all this. Maybe because it was much easier talking about dead cows and threatening notes than discussing anything that might have happened between them in the past.

His jawline tightened as he dropped the note back on the table. "That's one nasty piece of work. What does Wayne say about all this? Surely you've called him."

"I called him the first time I found a cow down in the pasture and a note in my mailbox, but he hasn't had much to say about it all." She told him about the sheriff's visit that morning and the two times he'd been out before.

"This morning all he seemed really bothered by was the heat," she said.

"It's August in Dusty Gulch. Wayne is a native here, so the climate can't come as a big surprise to him. He's still got to do his job even if it's hot and uncomfortable. Do you have any idea at all who might be behind this?" he asked.

She shook her head. "I really don't have a clue."

"Have you dated anybody recently and broken up with them?" he asked.

"I haven't dated anyone at any time since my husband's death," she replied. "I have no interest in dating. I have my son and my ranch, and that's all I want and need in my life." She raised her chin slightly. "I haven't had any real issues with anyone and can't imagine why somebody is doing this to me."

"Sounds to me like you need for Wayne to step

up his game and find out who is behind all this," he replied.

She released a small, dry laugh. "That goes without saying." She sobered quickly. "I've been having some trouble with some teenagers."

"What kind of trouble?" Jake asked and then took a sip of the cooling coffee.

"A bunch of them have been sneaking out here pretty regularly to use my barn as a party place late at night. I've caught them a couple of times and have chased them off, but I do wonder if maybe they're responsible for the notes and the dead cows as some form of revenge against me."

"Did you tell that to Wayne?" he asked.

"I did. I even gave him a couple of names of the kids, but I'm not sure he did any follow-up." She glanced at the clock on the wall, wanting Jake gone before Andy came home from school.

"I'll give Wayne a call and see if I can light a fire under him."

"Thanks, I would really appreciate that." She got up from the table, hoping he would take the hint and leave. Despite their fairly easy conversation, she was still uncomfortable in his presence. To her relief he got up as well, and together they walked to the front door.

"It was nice seeing you, Jake," she said.

He took a step closer to her. "It was good seeing you, too, Eva. You're even more beautiful than I remember." He lifted his hand, as if to stroke her hair, and then quickly dropped it back to his side.

For just a brief moment, their gazes locked, and in the depths of his dark eyes she saw something that half stole her breath away. It was something she remembered from those summer days and nights so long ago…a fiery desire that threatened to pull her in.

Shocked, she quickly took a step back from him and broke the eye contact. "I guess I'll see you around."

"Oh, you'll definitely be seeing me, and I intend to call Wayne as soon as possible and find out what's being done as far as these crimes against you."

"I really appreciate that."

"Can I get your phone number?"

She wasn't thrilled with him having her number, but if he was going to speak with Wayne on her behalf, then he should probably have it. She grabbed her cell phone, and he punched his number into hers and then set her up in his contact list.

"I'll call you after I speak with Wayne. I'm driving into town right now and will try to catch up with him."

"Thanks, Jake."

With a final last look at her, he was gone. She closed the door and leaned against it. For the first time since he'd walked into the house, she felt as if she could finally draw a full breath.

She hadn't ever expected to see him again—here

in her house or anywhere else. More than that, she hadn't expected the emotions the very sight of him had evoked in her.

An unexpected desire had punched her in the stomach the minute she had seen him. A desire coupled with a deep yearning for what might have been. And would now never be.

She still wasn't sure why he'd stopped by to see her. However, she did appreciate him talking to Wayne, because she knew having an Albright behind her would make the sheriff take things far more seriously.

But that was all she wanted from Jake Albright.

He was dangerous to her. He was dangerous to the life she had built here with her son. He had the money and power to destroy her, and she feared that's exactly what he would do if he ever found out Andy was his son.

AT EIGHT THIRTY the next morning, Jake got in his truck to drive back to Eva's. The day before he'd had a long talk with Wayne Black about what was going on at Eva's ranch. He'd let Wayne know that he wanted Wayne to keep him informed not only about anything else happening there, but also about exactly what Wayne was doing to investigate.

Wayne had called him earlier this morning to tell him that Eva had found two more mutilated cows in her pasture. Jake was meeting Wayne there to see for himself what exactly was going on.

He couldn't help the way his nerves grew taut as he thought of seeing Eva again. He'd realized yesterday that she was still a fire in his blood. Despite the years that had passed and all of his dating when he'd been out of the country, Eva had always been in the back of his mind, somehow keeping him from moving on in any meaningful way with any other woman.

He needed to possess her one last time to hopefully get her out of his head, out of his blood forever. His junior and senior years in school had been spent loving Eva, and he'd believed at the time she loved him back.

Hell, they had even held a mock wedding ceremony in the hayloft of her barn, where they had pledged to marry for real as soon as she graduated from high school. He had truly believed that she would be the woman in his life forever, that she would be his legal wife and have his children.

He would never love her again. She'd hurt him so badly. He would never forget that she'd betrayed the love he thought they'd once shared. One evening without any warning, she'd just told him she didn't love him, that she didn't want to see him anymore.

He could never forget that within months of breaking up with him she'd married Andrew Martin, a ranch hand who had worked for her and her father. Had she and Andrew been seeing each other while Jake had been wrapped heart and soul with her?

It was a question that had haunted him for all these years. What had he been lacking that a quiet ranch hand had to offer her? And why, after all this time, did it even bother him?

That was then and this was now, he reminded himself as he pulled into her long driveway. He parked and got out of his truck, then started toward the house but stopped as he saw her out by the barn.

She was in the process of saddling up a horse but paused as she saw him approaching. She was clad in a pair of jeans that fit tightly on what he knew were slim hips and long, shapely legs. Her blue blouse was a gauzy material that looked both cool and sexy as hell, and her long black hair was in a thick braid down her back that he immediately wanted to undo.

"I didn't expect to see you this morning," she said in greeting.

"Wayne called me and told me you have two more dead cows. Same thing as before?" As he drew closer to her, the faint breeze blew the familiar scent of her to him.

She nodded. "Although the note was a little different this time." She pulled the note from her back pocket and handed it to him.

He frowned and opened it to read, "Get out of town, bitch, or die." He handed it back to her as a rich anger swept over him. Whoever was responsible for this was not only messing with her livelihood, but more egregiously, they were terrorizing her. She had to be frightened by the notes, and this one was a definite escalation from the last one.

"Wayne better get some answers on this," he said

tersely. "This isn't just a nasty note—this one is definitely a threat."

"Oh, he'll take it all more seriously now," she said with obvious confidence.

"Why do you sound so sure about that? You haven't felt like he was taking it seriously before now."

"I didn't have an Albright standing with me before now," she replied.

"That shouldn't make a difference," he replied.

"Oh Jake, surely you aren't still so naive. You have to know your name wields a lot of power in this town." She reached down and grabbed the saddle at her feet and swung it up and over the horse's back. "It's always been that way."

"I guess you're planning on riding out into the pasture when Wayne gets here. Do you have a spare horse I could borrow?" he asked.

He didn't want to think about what she'd said about him being naive. Still, it wasn't right that his being here with her would make Wayne take the case more seriously. The sheriff should take every crime that happened in this town seriously, and he definitely should have been taking this seriously all along.

She disappeared into the barn and moments later returned with a large black mare who had a white marking on her nose that looked like a lightning bolt.

"This is Lightning," she said.

"Very appropriate name," he said with a grin. He

gestured toward her big dark mare. "And I suppose she's Thunder."

She returned his smile. "That's exactly right." Her beautiful smile lasted only a moment and then was gone. "The gear is in the second stall on the right. Help yourself to whatever you need."

By the time he grabbed what he needed and returned, she was already mounted on the back of her horse. For the next few minutes, he got his horse ready, and then he mounted as well.

"Seems like old times," he said, remembering how much they had always enjoyed horseback riding together in the past. They'd get out of school and then ride horseback on the ranch until it was time for her to start cooking dinner.

She looked out in the distance. "Those carefree days of youth are long gone," she replied. "And we'll never get them back."

He wasn't sure if he was imagining it or not, but her words sounded like a warning to him. But, before he could reply to her, two men came from around the side of the barn on horseback.

"Jake, this is Harley Graham, my foreman for the last seven years, and Jimmy Miller, who has worked for me for the past year," she said. "And this is Jake Albright. He's here to help with Sheriff Black."

"That man definitely needs some help," Harley, the older of the two, muttered halfway beneath his breath. "And it's nice to meet you, Mr. Albright."

"Jake," he replied. "Please call me Jake." Harley

looked like a man who'd worked in ranching his whole life. His face was weatherworn, and there was a quiet confidence about him.

Next to Harley, Jimmy looked like a young pup. Shaggy blond hair peeked out from beneath his black cowboy hat, and his bright blue eyes held an eagerness to please.

"Harley and Jimmy found the two cows this morning," Eva explained to Jake.

"Bad business going on around here," Harley said. "Somebody out there is trying to destroy Eva."

"Between all of us, we won't let that happen," Jake replied forcefully.

They all looked toward the road at the sound of a vehicle approaching. It was Wayne. He pulled up and parked and then left his car running and stepped out. "Looks like we're all ready to go," he said, as if he had been the one waiting for all of them. "You lead and I'll follow."

Eva looked at Harley, who gave a curt nod and then galloped away. The others quickly caught up with him as Wayne took up the rear in his car.

Jake rode just behind Eva, admiring her form in the saddle. He'd forgotten how good she looked on the back of a horse, like she'd been born there. Her slender back was straight, and her hips rolled easily with the horse's gait.

As always the smells of pasture and cattle were welcome to Jake. They rode past the pond where he and Eva had often fished together. He forced back the memories that threatened to erupt in his head.

He looked ahead and frowned. He could now see the two downed cows on the ground. The scent of blood and death hung in the still, hot air, and two buzzards circled lazily in the sky above.

They all dismounted next to the big animals and waited for Wayne to leave his car and join them. There was no question the cows' throats had been slashed, and there were bloody, butchered holes in their chests.

What in the hell was going on here? Who was behind this kind of madness? The taking of the hearts was particularly heinous. Why were they targeting Eva, and how much danger was she really in?

They all dismounted, and then Jake turned to look at Wayne. "What are you doing to find out who is responsible for this?"

Wayne shifted from one foot to the other. "This has been a tough thing for me to investigate. There have been no weapons left behind and no real clues for me to work with."

"Eva told me she mentioned some teenagers to you. Have you questioned them?" Jake asked.

"I really haven't had a chance yet," Wayne confessed.

"Get a chance today, Wayne. The note Eva got this morning is definitely a threat." Jake spoke forcefully.

He and Wayne had gone to high school together. Jake had always liked the man, but Wayne had been lazy in high school, and that trait seemed to have followed him into adulthood. Jake didn't want Eva to be a victim of what Jake suspected was Wayne's usual lethargy.

"I'll get on it as soon as I leave here," he said. He looked at Eva. "Is there anyone else you can think of that might have a grudge against you?"

Eva frowned. "I've been thinking about it, and I guess you might want to question Ben Wilkins."

"Who is he?" Jake asked.

"He's a ranch hand I had to fire about six months ago," she replied. "He's a heavy drinker and more often than not didn't show up for work. I thought we'd parted ways amicably, but who knows."

"I think he's working on the O'Brien spread now, although I haven't seen him around town lately. If I can find him, I'll have a chat with him as well," Wayne said.

"I just want all this to stop," Eva said. "I can't afford to lose my cattle, and nobody is going to make me leave town." She raised her chin. "This is my land, and nobody is going to terrorize me off it."

"You know you have our support," Jimmy said fervently. "I'd never let anything happen to you, Eva."

By the look in Jimmy's eyes as he gazed at Eva, it was obvious the young pup had a big crush on his boss. As long as he stayed in his own lane and didn't get in Jake's way, there would be no problem.

The group broke up. Wayne drove off with a

promise to come back later that evening, and Eva and Jake headed back to the barn, leaving Jimmy and Harley the distasteful duty of taking care of the dead cows.

As much as Jake would have loved to stay with Eva, by the time they unsaddled the horses and put them back in their stalls, it was time for him to head back home and get cleaned up for the appointment with his father's lawyer.

"Thanks for coming out this morning," she said as she walked him to his truck.

"Eva, I intend to be here for you until Wayne has solved this and somebody is in jail."

"That's really not necessary. I'm sure Wayne is going to step up and do his job," she replied. "I appreciate what you've done, but you're officially off the hook now."

She had no idea how badly he was on her hook, how much he wanted to taste her lips once again and feel her lithe body against his own. He wasn't about to walk away from her before he got what he wanted.

And since he had left Dusty Gulch all those years ago, Jake Albright always got what he wanted.

Chapter Three

As Eva finished up her morning chores, she tried to keep her mind off Jake. She hoped he wouldn't come around anymore. Just the sight of him stirred up too many memories, ones that were both exquisite and splendid and others that were too painful to entertain.

She ate a light lunch and then decided to put on some tomato sauce for spaghetti and meatballs for dinner. Even though the hot weather called for cold salads and sandwiches for the evening meals, Andy loved her spaghetti and meatballs. She tried to make it for him fairly regularly.

There had been a time when she would expect Jake to share the evening meal with her and her father. Her father had adored Jake and had treated him like the son he'd never had. She had loved the relationship the two had shared. It had killed her to end things with Jake not only for herself, but for her father as well.

He'd never asked her what had happened between her and Jake. She supposed he supported whatever decision she made in her dating life, and her father had respected her privacy on the matter.

She wasn't that girl anymore...the young girl who had believed anything was possible with love...that anything was possible with Jake.

The life choices she'd been handed had been decisions that had been necessary but difficult. They had been decisions she'd had to make with her head and not with her heart.

Other than the joyous birth of her son, her life had been built by moments of quiet contentment and respect for the man who had offered to marry her in order to give Andy his name.

Andrew Martin had been the one who had helped her through her grief over her father's unexpected death. That had been a time of fear...of complete uncertainty.

Jake was gone, and she'd been a pregnant eighteen-year-old with a ranch that was failing. Andrew had stepped in with an offer of marriage that had benefited them both at the time. And in the end, he had left her a life insurance policy that had helped her stay afloat around the ranch and put some money away in a college fund for Andy.

As the scents of garlic and tomatoes filled the kitchen, she sank down at the table and wished her father was alive. She needed to talk to somebody and say that the note today had frightened her even more than the others. *Get out of town, bitch, or die.*

Who could possibly entertain such utter hatred toward her?

She'd always kept a pretty low profile. She stayed busy working on the ranch and raising Andy. She went into town only when she needed supplies or if Andy had some activity, and she was always pleasant to the people she encountered.

So, who was behind all this? Although she took the death of her cattle very seriously, she wasn't sure how seriously to take the personal threats indicated in the notes.

Nasty notes couldn't hurt her. However, would the person writing the notes escalate and try to physically harm her? Kill her? She got up and stirred the sauce as troubling thoughts continued to fire through her brain.

Nobody had shown any interest in wanting her ranch. Nobody had stepped forward to offer to buy the place. She'd had no indication about anyone being interested in getting this land away from her. Her father had bought all these acres when he'd been nineteen years old, and he'd built the house they now lived in. Nobody was ever going to force her off this land.

So why was somebody obsessed with her leaving town?

At four o'clock she left the house and walked down the lane to the main road where the school bus would drop Andy. Even though it was only mid-August, school had started the week before due to the many snow days the kids often had off in the winter. As always, all bad thoughts fell away from her mind as she anticipated seeing her son.

The bus pulled up and Andy jumped off, his wide smile immediately contagious. "Hi, Mom. I got an A on my spelling test and can I spend the night with Bobby tonight? It's Friday night so we don't have school tomorrow. We already talked to his dad and he said he could pick me up and we'd go out for pizza for dinner and then we can rent a movie."

"Congratulations on the spelling test," she said and grabbed his hand to hold as they headed back to the house. "And you know I'll have to check all the details with Bobby's father. I'll have to make sure you and Bobby don't have him tied up somewhere and are forcing him to meet your demands."

Andy giggled. "You're silly, Mom."

"I'll still need to speak with Bobby's father," she replied, her heart warmed by her son's laughter.

"He said you can call him as soon as I get home from school. Bobby and I want to rent a scary movie tonight."

"Then I'm glad I won't be there with you. You know how much I hate scary movies."

"That's 'cause you're just an old fraidy-cat," Andy replied with a giggle.

"Oh yeah?" Eva released his hand and proceeded to tickle him.

He howled with laughter and took off running toward the house with her following in hot pursuit. "I made you spaghetti for dinner," Eva said once they were inside.

Andy frowned. "I guess I could stay and eat dinner here before going to Bobby's."

"Don't be silly. You can always have the spaghetti tomorrow night. You go pack your overnight bag and I'll give Bobby's father a call."

"Thanks, Mom. I love you," he said and then zoomed out of the kitchen and down the hallway toward his bedroom.

At five thirty Robert Stephenson pulled up with his son, Bobby. Bobby bounced out of the car, and the two boys bumped shoulders and then high-fived each other.

Robert was a handsome man with sandy brown hair and green eyes. Tragically, he had lost his wife three years ago to cancer. Eva never worried about Andy spending time at the Stephenson house. She knew Robert had rules and a parenting style that closely mirrored her own.

"Hi, Eva." He greeted her with a warm smile.

"Hey, Robert, are you sure you're ready for this?" She gestured toward the two energetic boys who were dancing around each other and fake fighting.

He laughed. "I think I can handle them. Maybe one evening the four of us could go out for some pizza together."

This wasn't the first time Robert had mentioned an outing including her. "Right now I'm staying really busy, Robert. It's really hard for me to get away."

She'd sensed that the man had a romantic interest in her. She wasn't interested in him, but she also didn't want to say or do anything that might mess up the boys' friendship.

"But Eva, everyone needs a break once in a while," he chided. "You know the old saying about all work and no play."

"I know, and maybe we can plan something sometime in the future," she replied noncommittally.

"I'd really like that," he replied. "Now, what time do you need your son home tomorrow?"

"Whatever time is convenient with you. I should be here all day."

Within minutes they were gone, and Eva was alone in the house. She ate spaghetti for dinner and then put the leftovers in the fridge and cleaned up the kitchen. Once that was done, she went into the living room and sank down on the sofa.

With a deep sigh, she reached up and unwound the braid in her hair, then used her hairbrush to stroke through the long strands.

It had been a long day, starting with the discovery of the two dead animals and the new note. She was exhausted not from any physical activity she'd done during the day, but rather from the simmering fear that buzzed continuously inside her head.

She'd never felt afraid here. She kept her father's shotgun loaded and in a gun safe in her bedroom, but she'd never had to take it out. Tonight, however, the silence of the house pressed in all around her as she thought of the notes she'd received.

She got up and checked to make sure the front door was securely locked and then went to the back door and did the same thing. Being a single woman with a young son, she had invested in good locks on the doors and windows when Andrew passed away.

The place didn't have central air, although she had air-conditioning units in the windows of the living room and both bedrooms. She only ran the one in her bedroom when it was really hot and there was no breeze coming into the second window in her room. Eventually she'd love to get central air, but right now that wasn't in her limited budget.

She closed and locked the windows in the kitchen and then returned to the sofa and turned on the television to fill the quiet.

It was a few minutes after eight when her phone rang, and she saw by the identification that the caller was Wayne. "Is it too late to make a house call?" he asked.

"Not at all, what's up?" she asked.

"I just wanted to come by and update you with what I've learned today. I'll be out there in about twenty minutes or so."

"Okay, see you then," Eva replied. She got up and reopened the kitchen windows to allow in the light evening breeze and then put on a pot of coffee.

She hoped the sheriff was bringing some answers. God, she hoped he was coming to tell her he'd identified the guilty person and that person was now behind bars. That was the only thing that would both answer her questions and halt the simmer of fear that had burdened her since the first cow and note.

About twenty minutes later, with the sun dipping low in the sky, Wayne arrived with Jake following in his truck right behind.

She was definitely not happy to see Jake, who was spending far too much time and energy in her business. And yet she had to confess she was grateful he'd initially gotten involved, since it had obviously lit a fire under Wayne's backside. But it was now time for him to go away.

"Wayne." She opened the door wider to allow in the lawman. "Jake, I didn't expect to see you here again."

"Expect to see me around here a lot," he replied as he followed Wayne through the living room and into the kitchen.

Now that's so not happening, she thought to herself as she followed them into the kitchen. But she couldn't exactly set Jake straight in front of Wayne. She would definitely speak to Jake once Wayne left.

"Ah, I smell fresh-brewed coffee," Wayne said as he sank down at the table.

"I know how much you like your coffee, Wayne," she replied. No matter the time of day or night, she rarely saw the man around town without a cup of java in his hand.

"None for me," Jake said.

She poured Wayne a cup and then joined the two men at the table. "I hope you have some good news for me, Wayne," she said.

He winced. "Well, I wouldn't go that far," he replied. "I just wanted to catch you both up on what I've done today." He shot a quick glance at Jake and then looked back at her. "I want you to know I'm taking this all very seriously."

"Then what do you have for us?" Jake asked.

When did she become "us" with Jake Albright? She tried not to look at him, even though she was acutely aware of him. His presence made the room feel too small and without enough air to get a full breath.

Wayne rose just enough to pull a notepad from his rear pocket. He opened it and flipped the pages in obvious self-importance. "The first person I spoke to this afternoon was Griff Ainsley."

"Who is he?" Jake asked.

"He's one of the teenagers who have been using my barn to party in," Eva explained. She'd given Wayne Griff's name after the first dead cow had been found. "He's a mouthy, disrespectful boy who has been in my barn with his friends more times than I can count. He seems to be the ringleader of all of them."

"So, what did he have to say?" Jake's jaw muscle tightened.

Wayne's cheeks dusted with color, and he kept his gaze on the notepad on the table in front of him. "He said Eva was a crazy woman. He told me that he and a couple of his friends had come out here at the beginning of the summer to see if Eva needed any part-time help. But she greeted them all with a gun and screamed at them to get off her property or she'd shoot them. After that he said he'd stayed away from here."

"He's such a liar," Eva replied sharply. "That certainly never happened, and the kids were out in my barn as recently as two weeks ago. I cleaned up the trash they left behind, like I always have to do. I'll admit I've confronted them before and I've screamed at them all, but never with a gun."

"So, what was his alibi on the nights that Eva's cattle were killed?" Jake asked.

"He was in bed asleep, and his parents backed him up." Wayne finally looked at Eva.

"Are they the kind of people who would lie for their son?" Jake leaned forward in his chair.

Wayne hesitated a long moment and then finally replied, "Yeah, they'd probably lie for him. He's their only kid. He's also the high school's star quarterback, and they're very proud of him. They definitely wouldn't want him to get in any trouble."

"So we don't know if this is the work of a bunch of teenagers or not," she replied flatly.

"Not at this point. I also don't think Ben Wilkins is responsible, either," Wayne said.

"He's the ranch hand I fired six months ago," Eva reminded Jake. "Why do you think he isn't responsible?" she asked Wayne.

"He quit the O'Brien ranch about two months ago and moved to Makenville," Wayne replied, referring to a nearby small town.

"That's only a twenty-minute drive from here," Jake said. "He could easily drive here, wreak havoc on Eva's ranch and then drive back. Did you interview him in person?"

"I didn't get a chance today, but it's on my to-do list for tomorrow." Wayne took a drink of his coffee.

"What about the notes? Have you been able to pull any fingerprints from them?" Jake asked.

"Not in the two I've checked so far. There were a few on them, but I'm guessing they were Eva's."

"You're guessing?" Jake looked at Wayne in disbelief. "Have you taken Eva's fingerprints so you can rule hers out?"

"Uh…not yet. Eva, maybe you can stop by the office sometime tomorrow and we can get that done," Wayne replied.

"I'll be glad to," Eva said. Finally something was being done. Even though Wayne hadn't brought any real answers with him, she did believe now he would do anything in his power to find the guilty person or persons. If nothing else, he wouldn't want to displease Jake.

Wayne took another drink of his coffee and then tucked the small notepad back into his pocket. "Right now I don't have a lot to go on, but I intend to keep digging for answers."

"I would expect nothing less from you, Wayne,"

Jake said. "Whoever is behind this needs to be caught and thrown into jail."

Wayne finished his coffee and then stood and looked at Eva. "I promise you I'm going to stay on top of this, but if you think of anyone else who could be doing this to you, you need to contact me immediately."

"I've twisted and turned my brain inside out trying to think of anyone who might have an issue with me, but other than the names I gave you, I can't think of anyone else." Eva and Jake also got up from the table, and the three of them headed back to the front door.

"I'll check in with you tomorrow after I've spoken to some more people," Wayne said.

She turned on her porch light, and they all stepped out of the house. "Thanks, Wayne," she said. "I'll probably be in sometime tomorrow afternoon to get my fingerprints taken."

"That works for me," he replied.

She watched as Wayne got into his car, and then she turned to look at Jake, who seemed to be in no hurry to head out. "I appreciate your help in this, Jake. But I told you this morning there's really no reason for you to be involved with this anymore."

"But Eva, I intend to stay involved." He took a step closer to her, and every muscle in her body tensed. "I'm worried about you, and I intend to be here for you until I know there's no more danger to you."

He took another step closer, now invading her personal space and bringing with him his familiar scent. "It's just been notes left in the mailbox and nothing more dangerous than that," she replied.

"But we can't know what might happen next, and that's what has me worried for you." His gaze bored into hers, and for a moment she couldn't breathe. "Right now it's just notes."

He looked at her now the same way he had then... when she'd been sixteen years old and they had been madly, crazy in love. His dark, sinful eyes beckoned her forward, to take the last small step between them and fall into his arms.

For just a brief, insane moment she wanted to fall. She wanted to be in his strong arms and feel his lips on hers. She remembered the magic, the all-consuming passion they had once shared, and there was a part of her that wanted to feel that again.

"I want you, Eva. I've never stopped thinking about you." His deep voice shot a wave of heat through her. Before she knew what was happening, he opened his arms and she fell into them as she parted her lips to receive his kiss...it was a fiery kiss that she'd desperately wanted.

It was still there...the desire that he'd always been able to evoke in her. It shocked her, and before he could deepen the kiss any more, she stumbled back from him.

"Jake, I'm not interested in going backward. Our past is gone and there's no place for you in my life now," she said.

His dark gaze held hers, and then his mouth moved into his sexy smile. "That's not what our kiss just told me. Good night, Eva."

Before she could say anything in response, he was gone, swallowed up by the darkness outside the illumination of the porch light. She went into the house and collapsed on the sofa, her body still warmed by the kiss they had shared.

She'd known Jake was a danger to her because of the secret of Andy, but she'd never dreamed that he'd be a danger to her because of her own desire for him.

She needed to stay away from him. Right now he felt as dangerous to her as the person who was mutilating her cattle and leaving the hateful notes.

She had once loved Jake Albright with all her heart and soul. He'd not only been her lover but also her best friend. She hadn't cared one bit about his family's money and power. She had loved the sweet, gentle boy who had aspired to ranch and love her forever.

The truth of the matter was she didn't trust herself with Jake. She had loved him ten years ago, and she was shocked to realize now that she had never really fallen out of love with him.

SUNDAY AFTERNOON JUSTIN ALBRIGHT was laid to rest. Most of the townspeople showed up to pay their final respects, but Jake had never felt so alone.

As he stared at the flower-adorned coffin and listened to the preacher drone on, extolling Justin

Albright's life, all Jake could think about were the years he'd lost with his father.

Even though his father had flown to Italy to visit Jake several times over the years, it hadn't been enough for Jake to feel the closeness he'd yearned for. And now would never have.

David and Steph stood next to him, but Jake wished Eva was beside him. Eva knew how much he'd loved his father, how badly he'd wanted a deeper, more meaningful relationship with the man he'd admired and loved. Eva would understand the depth of grief that now pierced through him.

The funeral seemed to last forever, and once it was over, dozens of people descended on the house with food and more condolences. David and Steph were gracious hosts, while Jake felt disconnected from everyone. He hung around for about an hour, and then he changed out of his suit and into more casual clothes and sneaked away to the stables.

He saddled up and then took off riding across the pasture, hoping to escape some of the grief that clung to him. His thoughts were scattered as the sun beat down hot on his shoulders. He rode hard and fast until he reached a large shade tree, where he pulled up and dismounted.

From this vantage point, he could see the herd of cattle in the distance. His father's will had left everything divided equally between his two sons, with an additional amount of money set aside for any grandchildren. He'd been grateful that David had agreed to let him run the ranching business and continue to manage the winery and David would take care of all the other businesses.

Jake had already spoken to David about potentially putting the winery on the market. They could sell it at an enormous profit and get out of the wine business altogether.

Running the ranching side of things was all Jake had ever wanted to do. He felt a real affinity for the land. There had been one man who had understood exactly how Jake felt, and that had been Eva's father.

He wished he'd been in town when Tom Taylor had died. He wished he'd been here for Eva, but instead he'd been in Italy, and apparently Andrew Martin had been the man who had helped Eva with her grief.

According to what he'd heard, it had been soon after that when Andrew and Eva had gotten married and not long after that she'd been pregnant.

Jake still had questions about that time. One night Eva had professed her deep and abiding love for him and they'd been planning their future together, and the next night she'd told him she didn't care anything about him and she never wanted to see him again.

She'd indicated that they couldn't go back in time, and while Jake would like some answers, he didn't want to go back for anything other than making love with her one last time. She might act like she's immune to him now, but the brief kiss they had shared told him much differently.

There was still something there between them,

something burning hot and wild, and he couldn't wait to explore that again. He would never forget how she'd broken his heart, but he had no intention of ever giving her his heart again.

Still, he was very concerned about the fact that somebody was targeting her. The dead cattle and the notes worried him, and from what he'd heard around town so far, she didn't have anyone to support her other than her two ranch hands.

With Eva still on his mind, he saddled up and headed back to the stables. He'd been gone long enough that all the well-wishers were gone from the house.

He showered and changed clothes and, feeling too restless to just hang around the house, he grabbed his truck keys and headed into town with no particular destination in mind.

Once he was on Main Street, he parked and took off walking at a leisurely pace in an attempt to get rid of the restlessness that had plagued him since the funeral. David had been right—the small town was growing, and there were many new businesses open since the last time Jake had been here.

It was past the dinner hour and not too many people were on the sidewalks, but the few who passed him nodded or offered their condolences about his father.

He smiled as he saw Benny Adams approaching from the other direction. Benny had been one of Jake's best friends in high school. "Hey, man,"

Benny said as he pulled Jake into a bear hug. He released him and took a step back. "I wanted to talk to you at the funeral today, but there were so many people around I couldn't get to you. I'm so sorry about your father."

"Thanks," Jake replied.

"So, what are your plans now that you're back?" Benny asked. "Are you going to hang around for a while before heading back to Italy?"

"I'm staying here for good. I've had enough of being on foreign soil. But tell me about you. Have you married? Do you have a family?"

"Yeah, I married Lori right out of high school." Benny grinned. "You know how that girl drove me crazy during our senior year—well, she's still keeping me crazy." Benny laughed.

"That's terrific. You have kids?"

"Yeah, two. I've got a boy who is six and a three-year-old daughter who Lori and I are convinced is the spawn of Satan. In fact, I'm on my way to the grocery store because the spawn of Satan wants chocolate milk before bed."

Jake laughed. "I'd love to get together with you and your family for dinner one night."

"Sounds good to me. What about you? From what I've seen in the occasional newspaper clippings, you look like you've been busy dating a lot of hot women and living it up in Italy. Any one of those women get you to the altar?"

"No, I'm still footloose and fancy-free."

"I'm going to hold you to that dinner. Lori is a great cook, and we'd love to have you over to our place."

"Just tell me when and where and I'll be there," Jake replied. The two men exchanged information, and then Benny hurried on down the sidewalk toward the grocery store.

Jake watched until he disappeared into the store. So, Benny had married his high school sweetheart and had a family. It was what Jake had once hoped for with Eva. He'd once believed that by now he'd be long married to her and they'd have a couple of children.

He sighed and continued down the walkway. He was just about to pass by an ice cream parlor when he halted in his tracks. Seated inside at one of the high round tables were Eva and her son, Andy.

Suddenly he had an overwhelming hankering for a strawberry ice cream sundae. He pushed open the door and entered the shop. "Eva," he greeted her. "And you must be Andy," he said to the young boy. "Hi, my name is Jake. I'm an old friend of your mother's."

"Cool, it's nice to meet you, Mr. Jake," the boy replied with a bright smile.

"I certainly didn't expect to see you here," Eva said, her gaze simmering with a hint of anger.

"I felt a little restless after all the events of the day and decided to come into town," he replied. "I was just passing by and thought I'd get some ice cream."

The anger in Eva's eyes softened. "I'm sure today was a difficult one for you," she said. She looked at her son, who appeared curious. "Jake's father died, and the funeral for him was today."

"I'm sorry, Mr. Jake," Andy said with sadness in his eyes...eyes that were shaped just like his mother's. "My dad died when I was only three years old. I don't remember being sad, but I'm sure I was, and I'm sorry if you feel sad."

"Do you think I'd feel better if I got some ice cream and sat here with you and your mom for a few minutes?" Jake asked.

"Maybe," Andy replied. "Mom and I are pretty nice."

"Then I'll just go get me some ice cream and be right back." Jake knew he was being a bit manipulative in forcing Eva to either make a scene in front of her son or accept his presence gracefully. But surely it couldn't hurt for them all to enjoy some ice cream together.

He got a strawberry sundae and then rejoined Eva and her son at their table. "So, what are the two of you doing out and about on a Sunday evening?" he asked.

"We're celebrating an A on a difficult spelling test," Eva said with a look of pride at her son.

"So, you're not only a handsome boy, but you're smart as well," Jake said. "What do you want to be when you grow up?"

"I want to raise cattle and work on the ranch just

like my mom," Andy replied. "But Mom says I've got to get my education before she turns things over to me."

"That sounds like good advice to me," Jake replied.

"What do you do, Mr. Jake?"

"I've been away for a while, but now I'm going to work on my family ranch and raise cattle."

"Cool," Andy said.

"Do you like to fish?" Jake asked.

"I've never been," Andy replied.

"What? There's a big pond right there in the pasture near your house and you've never fished in it?" Jake looked at Eva in surprise. Andy shook his head.

"It's one of those things we've just never made time to do," Eva said with a touch of guilt in her voice.

"Maybe I could take you fishing when you get home from school tomorrow if your mother agrees," Jake said.

Andy's face lit up with excitement. "Mom?"

"I guess that would be okay," she said, but her eyes communicated something far different than okay. They indicated to him that she was ticked off, but he was hoping that by tomorrow she'd have forgiven him. What could be wrong with taking a boy fishing? Especially one who had never been fishing before in his life?

The plans were made, and then the three of them

left the ice cream parlor together. "Do you feel better now, Mr. Jake?" Andy asked.

"I believe I do. Thank you for letting me spend some time with you and your mom," Jake replied.

"You can always spend time with us," Andy replied with a big smile.

"We'll start tomorrow with that fishing date."

"Go ahead and get in the truck, Andy," Eva said.

He ran to a red pickup parked in front of the shop, and Eva turned to Jake.

"Have you heard anything new from Wayne?" he asked, hoping to circumvent the tongue-lashing he suspected he was about to receive from her.

"No, and don't think I'm going to get distracted by you asking me that. If you think you're going to somehow get closer to me by getting closer to my son, you'd better think again." Her eyes snapped with anger as her chin rose. "Andy isn't some pawn in whatever game you might be playing."

God, she looked so beautiful in her mother-bear ire. "Trust me, Eva, I'm not playing a game, and the last thing I'd ever want to do is hurt your son."

"I'm warning you, you'd better not, Jake."

"I'm just taking him fishing, Eva. Don't make it a bigger deal than it is."

"Just remember what I said. I don't want him hurt." She gave him no chance to reply but rather turned and walked to her truck.

Instead of the restlessness that had filled him before, he was surprised by a wave of heartache that pierced through him. In another life and time, Andy could have been his son.

Andy should have been his son with Eva. Jake would have taken his son fishing. He would have taught him how to tie a rope and make a lasso. He would have spent time with his son and created the male bonding relationship that a father and son should have.

He wouldn't have spent his time behind a desk, consumed by profit and loss statements and making more and more money, like his father had done.

With a deep sigh, Jake got into his truck, a strange wistfulness riding with him all the way home.

Chapter Four

Eva woke up the next day in a foul mood. The cause of that mood? Jake Albright. She didn't like the fact that he was attempting to worm his way into her life by going through her son. It hadn't helped that Andy had been beside himself with excitement about the fishing date over breakfast.

He'd asked her about bait and different kinds of fish, and each question had only made her feel more guilty for not taking the time to take him fishing before now.

At least there had been no dead cows discovered this morning and no threatening notes in the mailbox. There was also no trash in the barn, indicating none of the kids had partied there the night before.

Of course, it had been a Sunday night and they all did have school today. But they had partied on school nights in the past. Unfortunately, the barn was too far away from the house for her to hear them whenever they arrived in the night.

The only times she'd caught them were when she'd

stayed awake and sat at the front window. The idea that Griff would say she had ever greeted the teenagers with a gun was absolutely ludicrous.

She did have a big stick she kept in the hallway closet, and she had carried it with her into the barn when the kids had been there for her own protection. But that stick was a far cry from a gun.

It wasn't that she was a big party pooper—she just didn't want a bunch of kids drinking and whatever else in her barn. First of all, they were trespassing, but equally important, she was afraid somebody was going to get hurt eventually. Not only would she feel terrible if one of them were injured, but she also didn't need the liability such an accident might cause.

At three o'clock she sank down at her table with a fresh cup of coffee. As her gaze landed on Andy's picture, a whirlwind of thoughts shot through her head.

She knew her son yearned to have a strong male figure in his life. It was the one thing Eva hadn't been able to give to him. After Andrew died, she hadn't wanted to date anyone. Her sole focus had been the ranch and her son. And nothing had changed since then. She still didn't want to date.

But she did wish Andy had a male in his life who could give him a man's perspective on life, a man who would take him fishing and to rodeos. She'd tried to be both mother and father to her son, but she knew there was no way she could make up for the lack of a father figure.

She certainly didn't want that person to be Jake. It had been the Albright power that had torn her and Jake apart, and she couldn't forget that now Jake had that wealth and power.

Thank God Andy had her features. She'd feared Jake and her son meeting, but Jake didn't seem to have any suspicions about Andy's paternity.

Eva had only lied to her son once, and that was when she'd told Andy his birthday. She'd moved Andy's birthday celebrations back three months in order to keep the secret of Andy being Jake's. Thankfully nobody in town had ever questioned it, and everyone believed Andrew was Andy's father. The only person who had known the truth was Andrew.

She would go to her grave with the secret of Jake being Andy's father. Just as she would go to her grave with the secret of what part Justin Albright had played in their breakup.

She knew how much Jake had loved and adored his father, and she would never tell him anything that would take that away. Even after all these years, she still cared enough about Jake not to do that to him.

The crunch of gravel announced the arrival of the devil himself. Andy wouldn't be home for another twenty minutes or so, and if Jake thought he was going to spend those minutes with her, then he had another thought coming.

She opened her front door as he got out of his truck. "Andy won't be here for another twenty minutes. Feel free to hang out here by yourself."

His eyes twinkled with amusement. "What's the matter, Eva? Afraid to spend a little time with me?"

"Of course not," she replied, instantly heated by his taunt. The minute she stepped out on the porch and closed the door behind her, she realized she'd given him exactly what he wanted.

"Beautiful afternoon for a little fishing," he said as he gestured to a tackle box, a cooler and two fishing rods that were in his truck bed. "You and I used to catch some big catfish out of your pond. Remember how we'd sit together on the little dock with our poles in the water as the sun set?"

His smile seduced her to remember that time with him, when they'd talked about everything from a simple wedding in the barn to what they would name their kids.

There was no way she was letting him into her head. "There should be plenty of big catfish left in the pond, since it hasn't been fished for years."

"Your son seems like a good kid," he replied.

"He's an awesome kid." As always, a wealth of pride rose up inside her as she thought of her son. "He's been a real joy from the moment he was born."

"You've obviously done a great job with him."

For a moment the warmth of his gaze felt welcome. She'd been alone for so long, and as she looked into his eyes, she remembered not only the love of the boy he had been, but also that he'd once been the keeper of her secrets and the builder of her dreams.

The rumble of the school bus approaching in the

distance snapped her out of the momentary lapse. "That will be Andy now." She began walking down the lane, and Jake fell into step beside her.

"I ran into Benny last night," he said. "Do you ever hang out with any of the old gang from high school?"

"I really don't have time to hang out with anyone." When she'd learned she was pregnant, she'd stopped seeing all her friends from school for fear they would know she was carrying Jake's child. Then there had been a baby to care for, an ill husband and her father's death.

Before Jake could ask her any more questions, the bus pulled to a halt and Andy got off. He hurried toward them, sheer excitement shining from his eyes and a happy bounce to his steps.

"Mr. Jake, you're here!" Andy smiled up at Jake.

"Well, of course I'm here. We have a fishing date," Jake replied as the three of them headed to the house. "Did you forget about that?"

"Heck, no. I just wasn't sure you'd really come," Andy replied. "But I want to catch a big fish."

Jake laughed. "And I want you to catch a big fish."

Eva's heart squeezed tight as she watched the interplay between her son and Jake. It was obvious Andy already had some hero worship going on.

She feared this relationship. She didn't want Andy to get attached to a man who would never have a place in her life. But it was too late to stop this afternoon of the two of them fishing together from happening.

"I've got bottles of water in the cooler, along with a container of big, fat worms," Jake said when they reached his truck.

"Worms?" Andy nodded his head. "Mom told me that worms are the best bait for catching a big cat-fish."

"Your mom is right. That's the best bait for catch-ing a big fish," Jake replied. "Are you going to be able to put a wiggling worm on a hook?"

"Of course," Andy replied confidently. "I'm not a wimp."

Jake laughed and reached out and ruffled Andy's hair. "I knew you weren't a wimp the first time I saw you." Andy beamed up at Jake.

"Then I guess I'll see the two of you later," Eva said.

She watched as the man who had once owned her heart and the boy who held her heart completely got into the truck and drove down the pasture lane to-ward the pond. For a brief moment, she wanted to run after them.

She wanted to sit on the edge of the dock with them. Fishing wasn't just about catching a big one. It was sitting together and talking quietly about any-thing and everything that popped into your head.

It was relaxing and talking and laughing together and building stronger bonds with the people who shared the dock with you. It was about a couple hours in time where nothing was important and worry was near impossible.

With a sigh, she turned and headed back to the house. The last thing she needed or wanted was to spend any more bonding moments with Jake.

She had spent the last ten years not only being angry with his father but also harboring what she knew was a bit of irrational anger toward Jake. Even though she had been the one forced to break up with him, he hadn't fought for her. He hadn't tried to change her mind. Instead he'd been on the next plane to Italy, and as far as she knew, he had never looked back.

After that, she'd always wondered if she'd been nothing but the cliché of a rich boy's toy for a couple of summers of sex. And in that hurt was the desire to keep herself in a place where he could never, ever hurt her again.

Instead of heading directly into the house, she went around to the back and picked a handful of big, ripe tomatoes to slice up for sandwiches for dinner.

As she worked, dark clouds began to gather in the southwestern sky, and the air thickened with additional humidity. She hoped the fishing didn't get interrupted by a pop-up thunderstorm. They could be fairly common at this time of year.

She carried the tomatoes through the back door and placed them in the kitchen sink to wash. Although it wasn't her intention for Jake to eat dinner with them, she had plenty of ham and cheese in case

Andy insisted his fishing buddy share the evening meal of sandwiches and chips.

The clouds had thickened even more, making for a false twilight, but so far there had been no lightning, thunder or rain. However, the wind had definitely picked up.

Her father had always told her the fish bit best when it was cloudy, and she hoped Andy was pulling out fish left and right.

A loud bang sounded several times from the front of the house. She hurried into the living room and peered out the front window. She saw nothing amiss.

The wind had probably found that loose shutter outside her bedroom window and smacked it against the house. She made herself a mental note to hammer it down in the next couple of days. She returned to the kitchen and busied herself by setting the table for two.

She flipped on the kitchen light to ward off the darkness caused by the clouds overhead, grabbed a soda from the fridge and then sat at the table to wait for the fishermen's return.

What were Jake and Andy talking about while they sat on the dock together? Was her son sharing thoughts and emotions with Jake that Andy hadn't shared with her? She shook her head to cast these thoughts out of her head, knowing she was being foolish.

She hoped that if Andy had some questions or issues he wasn't comfortable asking his mother, then he would ask those questions of Jake. She trusted

Jake to give her son good answers to whatever Andy might ask.

She wasn't sure how long she'd been sitting when, to her surprise, Jake's pickup pulled to a halt in front of the back door.

The two entered the kitchen. "Mom, I caught four big fish," Andy said, his eyes twinkling with excitement. "It was so cool. I had to fight to reel them in. Right, Mr. Jake?"

"Right," Jake replied. There was a tension radiating from Jake—a troubling tension. Had something happened with Andy? Had he misbehaved or back talked? Even as she thought it, she couldn't believe her son would ever be that kind of boy.

"But we let them go," Andy continued. "Mr. Jake said to let them go so they can get even bigger and we can catch them again. Catch and release, right, Mr. Jake?"

"That's right," Jake replied.

"Did you behave for Mr. Jake?" Eva asked her son.

"He did," Jake replied and smiled, but the smile didn't quite reach his eyes. "He turned out to be a terrific fisherman. And now why don't you go into the bathroom and wash up?"

"Okay." Andy raced out of the kitchen.

The minute he left, Jake turned to Eva, his gaze dark. "We need to call Wayne."

"Why? What's happened?" Her heart skipped a beat.

"One of your missing cow hearts has shown up."

A gasp escaped Eva. "What? Where?" Fear sizzled through her veins.

"Hanging from your front porch rail."

Eva stared at him in horror. Now she understood why he had driven around to the back door. It had been in an effort to keep Andy from seeing anything disturbing.

"Before we call Wayne, let me make Andy a sandwich and get him settled in his bedroom," she said.

"We should call him before it starts to rain," Jake replied. "The clouds have definitely thickened up."

"Just give me five minutes." Eva quickly made Andy a sandwich, added potato chips to his plate and had it ready by the time he returned to the kitchen.

"You can eat in your bedroom and play your video games until bedtime," she told him.

"Really?" Andy took the plate from her. "You never let me play my games on a school night."

"Tonight is the exception to the rule," Eva replied.

"Cool. Thank you, Mr. Jake, for taking me fishing. I hope we can do it again soon," Andy said.

Jake smiled. "We'll definitely do it again soon."

Andy took his plate and then disappeared into his bedroom. Eva headed for the front door, with Jake close behind her. Her heart beat the rhythm of dread as she anticipated what she was going to see.

The minute she stepped out on the porch, the wind whipped her hair around her head, and a bolt of lightning split the darkness of the clouds.

Even though she'd thought she was mentally prepared, she wasn't. There was no way she could have prepared herself for what she saw.

The cow's heart was stabbed through with a knife and dripped with blood. A note was next to it, appearing to have been written with the blood from the heart.

"Die, bitch."

It was a grotesque sight, made more horrifying by the fact that the person who threatened her had sneaked so close…had been bold enough to invade her personal space by coming up onto her porch.

She jumped, and a small cry escaped her lips as thunder boomed overhead. Jake threw his arm around her shoulder and pulled her close. Instead of pulling away from him, she leaned closer into him.

"Die, bitch." The words echoed in her head over and over again as she stared, almost mesmerized by the note next to the horrible bloody heart.

"Come on, let's get inside and call Wayne," Jake said gently and tightened his arm around her.

With her heart still pounding and fear tightening her stomach muscles, she prayed that this time Wayne would find something that would identify who was behind these attacks…before whoever was behind it made good on the threat.

JAKE STOOD ON the porch with Wayne and his deputy, Phil Barkley. Jake had insisted Eva stay in the house with her son while the men took care of the evidence gathering. There was no reason for her to see this atrocity again.

"That had to have been frozen," Jake observed as Phil took photos of the heart.

"Maybe, although it's sick to think about somebody…anybody in Dusty Gulch tearing the heart out of an animal and then putting it in their freezer," Wayne said. "It's hard to believe somebody in Dusty Gulch is behind any of this. It's the sickest thing I've ever seen."

"I just want to know who is targeting Eva and why," Jake replied.

"Let's hope this time the person made a mistake. Hopefully I can get something from the knife that was left behind," Wayne replied. "It's got a nice carved handle."

"Looks like it's handmade," Jake observed. "You know anybody who does that kind of work around here?"

"Not off the top of my head," Wayne replied. "But I'm not much of a knife guy."

"At least the rain held off," Jake said. Lightning had split the night sky and thunder had boomed overhead, but there hadn't been a drop of rain so far.

He watched as Wayne and Phil pulled on plastic gloves and then removed the knife and two ordinary nails that held the note in place. They then caught the heart as it fell into a plastic evidence bag. The knife, the nails and the note were also bagged as evidence, and then Phil left with the items.

Jake and Wayne spent the next twenty minutes walking the area around the porch and looking for anything that might provide a clue as to the identity of the perpetrator. However, they found nothing. Unfortunately the ground was too dry to give up a single footprint or tire track, and they didn't even know in what direction the perp had come from.

"I need to get back inside to Eva," Jake finally said.

"I'll head in with you. I need to get an interview with her on the record," Wayne replied. "I want to do everything strictly by the book, so when we catch this creep, the district attorney can put him away for a long time."

Together the two men went back into the house, where Eva sat on the edge of the sofa. She jumped up as they came in. "I made coffee," she said. Jake eyed her worriedly. Her eyes were slightly glazed, and she was pale. She appeared small and more vulnerable than he'd ever seen her. "Let's go into the kitchen, and I can get Wayne a cup of coffee."

She led the way, and as the two men sat at the table, she got Wayne a cup of the fresh brew and offered Jake a soda, which he declined.

Finally the three of them were seated, and Wayne took out his notepad and a small recorder. "Do you mind if I record your statement?" he asked.

"No, not at all," Eva replied.

"I just can't believe somebody had the nerve to do this while I was here," Jake said.

"Unless you specifically told somebody, nobody would have known you were here. Your truck was down by the pond and wouldn't have been visible from the road or the house," Eva said.

Jake was grateful to see a bit of color returning to her cheeks, and her gaze was becoming more clear and focused. "I didn't tell anyone I was coming here," he replied.

Wayne turned on his recorder and focused on Eva. "Do you have any idea what time this happened?"

"I'm not sure, but I heard a couple of bangs coming from the front of the house around six o'clock or so. I thought it was the wind banging one of the shutters that are loose." She frowned. "I looked outside, but I didn't see anything. If only I'd come all the way out of the house immediately when I heard it, maybe I could have caught the person."

"Thank God you didn't run out of the house," Jake replied. "Who knows what might have happened if you'd encountered the person?" The very thought of Eva interacting with the perp clenched Jake's stomach muscles and made him feel ill.

Minutes later, after Wayne had asked all his questions, Eva and Jake walked the lawman to the front door. "Hopefully the knife is going to be the key in breaking this case wide-open," he said. "It's unusual, and I'm going to home in and see what I can learn about it. I'll be in touch in the next day or two to let you know what we find out."

"At least Wayne seems to be stepping up his

game," Jake said when Wayne was gone. "Where is Andy?"

"He's sleeping. I think all the heat and excitement of fishing completely wore him out. I tucked him into bed while you and Wayne were outside. I just hope Wayne really can figure something out from the knife," she replied and then collapsed onto the sofa. To his surprise, she patted the sofa next to her. "Will you sit with me for a while?" There was a soft plea in her eyes that let him know she was still frightened.

"Of course. I should just move in here to keep you safe." He sank onto the sofa next to her.

She released a small laugh. "Jake, I asked you to stay for a little while, not to move in with us." Her laughter faded. "This whole thing is frightening, but the locks on my windows and doors are good ones, and I have a big stick and a shotgun in case I get really scared about somebody coming inside the house."

That moment of vulnerability she'd displayed earlier was gone. However, he knew she must be entertaining residual fear in the fact that she'd asked him to hang around for a while longer. If nothing else, the note written in blood had to have terrified her. It had certainly scared the hell out of him for her.

"It was fun taking Andy fishing for his first time," he said, knowing that talking about her son would ease some of her anxiety. "He was so excited about everything. He baited his own hook like a champion, and by the time we left the pond, he was casting out like a real pro."

A whisper of a smile curved her lips…lips that even under these circumstances he wanted to cover with his own. "I appreciate you taking him. I should have taken him a long time ago, but it was just one of those things that I kept putting off."

"So, tell me about your husband. Were you happy in the marriage?"

She hesitated a moment and then nodded her head. "Yes, I was happy. Andrew was one of the most gentle and truly good men I've ever known."

Jake's heart quickened slightly. "Eva, I just need to ask…were you seeing him while we were dating?"

Her eyes narrowed. "Do you really believe I'm the kind of woman who would do something like that? You do me a disservice by even asking that. The answer is no. At that time Andrew was just a ranch hand I occasionally saw working out in the pastures. And then my father died."

Her eyes filled with sadness, and she took a moment before continuing. "I was eighteen years old and utterly lost in my grief. I didn't know anything about how to run this place, and I felt so alone. Andrew stepped up and not only helped me through my grief, but also taught me what I needed to know about running this place and surviving here on the ranch my father had loved."

"I wish I had been here to help you with your grief," he replied. How he wished he had been the

one she'd leaned on and cried to, how he wished he'd been the one she'd depended on during that terrible time in her life. "So, why did you break up with me, Eva?"

She released a deep sigh. "Does it really matter now? I told you before, Jake, I don't want to rehash the past. It's over and done with, and we can't go back and rewrite history. Besides, I'm far more concerned about my future right now."

Her response didn't answer his question, but she was right. In the grand scheme of things, what did any of it really matter now? It was obviously his problem that he hadn't quite been able to get over her. Maybe by spending more time with her now, he'd realize they had never been meant to be together.

"I saw pictures of you on dates in Italy. None of those beautiful women managed to tie you down?" she asked.

"No, I wasn't even particularly serious with anyone over the last ten years. I found most of those beautiful women exceedingly boring."

A small laugh escaped Eva. "I find that hard to believe."

"It's the truth," he protested with a laugh of his own. "I really had nothing in common with any of them. They saw me as an heir to a fortune, but when I tried to tell them about my desire to ranch in Dusty Gulch, Kansas, their eyes glazed over and they stopped listening to me. It's hard to build a relationship with somebody when you can't talk about your real hopes and dreams."

He'd wanted to feel the same deep connection... the same passion for another woman that he'd once felt for Eva, but so far he hadn't found it with anyone else.

He suddenly realized how close they sat to each other, close enough that he could smell the spicy scent of her. He could feel the warmth of her radiating toward him—a warmth that had always both comforted and excited him at the same time.

Their gazes locked, and he felt himself falling into the beautiful violet depths. He was eighteen years old again, and in his eyes she was the most beautiful girl in the entire school, in the entire world.

Her long hair held the sheen of fine silk, begging him to stroke his fingers through the thick strands. His chest tightened, and he leaned closer to her.

Her eyes darkened, and she released a small gasp and sprang to her feet. "It's been a long day, Jake. I really appreciate you hanging out for a little while, but I'm fine now and I think it's time for us to say good-night."

Jake got up from the sofa, feeling as if he was reluctantly leaving behind a wonderful dream. "Are you sure you'll be all right? I could always bunk right here on the sofa for the rest of the night."

"Thanks, but I'll be fine." She walked with him to the front door. "Now that the initial shock is over, I'm okay."

"You'll call me if anything else happens or if you just get frightened?" he asked. She hesitated a moment and then nodded.

He lifted her chin with his fingers so he could look one last time into her beautiful, long-lashed eyes. "Promise me, Eva," he said.

"I promise." She stepped back from him. "Good night, Jake."

He told her good-night and then stepped out on the porch. She closed and locked the door behind him. His gaze shot directly to the place where the heart had hung.

Was somebody just terrorizing her with no desire to actually harm her? His hands tightened into fists at his sides. Who was doing this to her? Why would anyone do this to her? Would this escalate into something deadly?

There was no question that he was worried about her. However, he didn't believe anything more would happen tonight. He left the porch and headed for his truck.

It had been a long day, with lots of emotions to process. He'd truly enjoyed his time with Andy. The boy was bright and funny and had been eager to please. It was obvious he longed for a father figure in his life and missed the father he could barely remember.

Jake got in his truck but remained sitting without starting the engine as his tangled thoughts attempted to unwind. He'd seen the heart the minute he had pulled up toward the house and had immediately detoured around to the kitchen door in hopes that Andy wouldn't see the monstrosity. He didn't want Andy's memory of his first day fishing to be tainted. Hell, he never wanted a kid to see something like that.

He'd come here initially because he'd wanted to make love with Eva one more time...because maybe he'd wanted a bit of revenge on her for breaking his heart so many years ago.

But tonight something had changed in him. His desire for her was still there, as strong as it had ever been. But as he'd talked about sharing hopes and dreams, he'd remembered that he'd had that with Eva.

He still loved her. He was still in love with her. There was no doubt in his mind that she had loved him once. He didn't know exactly what had gone wrong between them, but none of that mattered now.

More than anything, he wanted to keep her safe from any and all danger—and he wanted her to love him again.

Chapter Five

"That kind of knife is sold at a couple of convenience and cigarette stores around the immediate area," Wayne explained. Lines of exhaustion creased the lawman's face, the lines made more prominent by the morning sun that danced through Eva's kitchen windows.

"We got lucky in that they are handmade by a man named Riley Kincaid, who lives out on a ranch about twenty miles from here. Unfortunately, I haven't had a chance to follow up on any of this, because old man Brighton was murdered in his sleep last night."

Both Eva and Jake released gasps of surprise. "How?" Jake asked.

"What about his wife? Is Sadie all right?" Eva leaned forward, horrified by this news. Walter Brighton and Sadie were fixtures around town. They had been married for fifty years, and they took afternoon walks together in town and greeted each person they passed with warmth. They often sat on the bench in front of the post office or could be seen having an early dinner at the café.

"Sadie is fine, but needless to say, she is very shaken up by this," Wayne replied. "Walter was stabbed sometime in the middle of the night while he slept."

"Where was Sadie when all this happened?" Jake asked. He looked so handsome this morning, clad in a navy blue T-shirt and a pair of jeans.

"Apparently Sadie slept in one of the other smaller bedrooms in their house due to Walter's loud snoring. She didn't see or hear anyone. She found Walter just after sunrise this morning when she went to wake him for the day. My point is right now all my men are assigned to the murder case, and I need to get back over to the scene of the crime as soon as possible. And that means it's going to be some time before I can speak to Riley Kincaid or follow up on any of the stores that sell the knife." He shook his head ruefully. "I'm sorry, but I've got to focus on this murder case right now."

"Wayne, we completely understand. How about Eva and I check out the convenience stores that sell the knife and speak to this Kincaid guy?" Jake asked.

Wayne sighed in obvious relief. "It would be real helpful if you two did the initial legwork," he said. "We need to find out who might have bought one of those knives recently. It looked brand-new. Unfortunately there were no prints on it, but if you remember, Jake, it had a wolf carved into it."

"Trust me, I remember," Jake replied.

"We'll see what we can find out by talking to these people," Eva said. Although she was ambivalent about spending any more time alone with Jake, the bloody heart and the new note had truly frightened her.

She would dance with the devil if it brought her closer to discovering who was behind the threats. And in this case, her devil was Jake.

She knew he could get answers where she might not be able to. His name not only commanded a lot of respect, but also a bit of fear. Storekeepers would speak to him because the Albrights owned most of the stores. Yes, she would dance with him in this investigation, but she couldn't let him in on a personal level.

Last night had proven just how dangerous he was to her. There was a part of her that ached with desire for him, a place that wanted to go back to that simpler time when they were just two teenagers madly in love with each other.

But going back in time wasn't possible, and having any kind of a personal relationship with Jake wasn't an option. She needed him right now to be her partner in helping to solve the mystery of the threats against her. But that was all she needed him for.

"I'll warn you, from what I hear this Kincaid fellow is a bit of an eccentric old coot." Wayne gave them Kincaid's address and then stood from the kitchen table. "All I ask is that you keep track of who you talk to and what they say. As soon as we get on top of this murder case, I'll have everyone in the station working on who is terrorizing you, Eva."

"Thanks, Wayne." Eva and Jake walked him to the front door. There was no question Eva was disappointed that Wayne couldn't get his men to investigate her case right now. But she certainly couldn't blame him for needing to investigate a murder that had just taken place the night before, and she knew how small Wayne's department and resources were.

"Want to take a ride?" Jake asked the minute Wayne had left.

"Where are we going?" she asked.

"How about we go talk to an eccentric old man about a knife?"

She nodded. "I'm in, as long as I'm back here by three forty-five or so when Andy gets off the bus."

"Then let's see how much investigating we can get done before then."

Minutes later they were in Jake's truck. The scent inside the cab cast her back in time—the pleasant smells of leather polish, his fresh-scented cologne and the familiar aroma that was in all her memories as just being Jake's.

Before they'd left her house, she'd grabbed a notebook in order to keep track of whom they spoke to and what they were told. She wanted to provide a clear and complete record for Wayne to use when he followed up.

"I can't believe Walter was murdered," she said once they were underway. "I can't even remember the last time Dusty Gulch had a murder. And who on earth would want to hurt poor Walter?"

"I wouldn't have a clue. Hopefully Wayne will be able to solve it quickly," Jake replied.

"I can't imagine who he'll even find as a suspect. I've never heard of Walter exchanging cross words with anyone." Just like she really didn't have a clue who any real suspect was in her own case.

It bothered her that the person who was terrorizing her could be somebody she saw often, somebody who smiled at her and was pleasant to her and yet hid this kind of evil hatred toward her.

Jake rolled down his window partway even with the air conditioner blowing from the truck vents. Immediately the scents of dusty heat and pastures filled the truck's interior.

"Ah, I missed the smell of the pastures while I was away," he said. "I also missed this scenery."

"But I've heard wine country is quite beautiful," she replied.

"Oh, it is, but it wasn't the sights or smells of home." He drew in a deep breath. "Now this looks and smells like home."

She wanted to ask him why he had flown to Italy the day after their breakup, but she knew the answer. His father would have orchestrated that to keep the two young lovers as far away from one another as possible. And Jake would have done anything to gain his father's approval.

"If you were so homesick, why did you stay away for so long?" she asked. Even in profile he was an extremely handsome man. She turned her gaze away from him and instead gazed out the front window.

"My father depended on me to run the wine business. He trusted me, and I didn't want to disappoint him. He thought I needed to be there and so I stayed, but I'm glad to be back here now."

"I have to admit, I'm glad you're here now. Otherwise Wayne would still be giving me the runaround," she replied.

"Wayne's not a bad guy—he's just lazy and needs somebody to push him occasionally," Jake replied.

"He'll have his hands full now with the murder." Eva shook her head. She still couldn't believe somebody had murdered Walter in his sleep.

For a few minutes, they rode in a comfortable silence. Hopefully Riley Kincaid kept a record of what stores carried his knives and who might have bought them directly from him. And hopefully one of those names was the person who was tormenting her.

"Tell me more about your husband."

She turned to look at him, surprised by his question. "What do you want to know about him?"

"Was he good to you?"

Eva's heart squeezed tight as she thought of Andrew. "He was very good to me."

"I'm glad. I heard he died of pancreatic cancer. That must have been very tough on you."

"It was. It's a brutal disease." It had been torture to watch Andrew suffer. In the end she'd been grateful that he'd finally passed to escape the ravages of the cancer. She'd been holding his hand when he'd finally taken his last breath.

"I'm so sorry you had to go through that," Jake said.

"I knew he was sick when I married him. Part of our arrangement was that I would be there for him to the end so he wouldn't have to die all alone. His parents were dead and he had no siblings. He really had nobody in his life except me."

"You said it was part of your arrangement." Jake shot her a curious look, and Eva cursed herself for saying as much as she had. "What do you mean by an arrangement?"

"Nothing," she replied quickly. "I just meant that when you marry somebody, you take a vow to be there in sickness and in health."

Thankfully that seemed to end his curiosity. He slowed the truck as they approached the turnoff on a narrow, two-lane country road. "This guy definitely lives out in the middle of nowhere."

"I wish somebody had been able to give us a phone number so we could call ahead to let him know we're coming," she replied. Wayne had told them that he had no phone contact for the man. He had a primitive web page up showcasing his knives but only an email address for contact.

"Let's just hope he got the email we sent," Jake replied. Before they had left her house, she had emailed Riley to let him know they were coming. Unfortunately there was no way for them to know how often the man read his email.

Once again they fell silent, although this silence felt charged with energy. She wasn't sure what Jake was feeling at the moment, but there was definitely a slight edge of desperation that tightened her chest.

She'd been living with her own personal nightmare for the past three weeks. From the moment she'd found her first dead cow and the first note in her mailbox, there had been a chill deep in her bones that grew colder with each new discovery. She was desperate for answers and hoped the knife maker would have them for her.

Jake pulled the truck to a halt and peered down the road that led to their right. Calling it a road was a stretch—it was little more than a dirt path through trees that encroached on either side.

"I think that is the driveway," he said.

"It looks more like a deer trail," she replied.

He turned into it and instantly hit a big pothole. "It's a bumpy deer trail. Hold on to your seat."

He had to crawl down the road as he attempted to miss the worst of the bumps. He also had to swerve slightly to avoid hitting a rabbit and then several squirrels that scurried across the road in front of them.

The air coming in through his window, rather than smelling of sweet pastures, now smelled of something dark and mysterious. The morning sunlight disappeared, trapped by the canopy of thick tree branches overhead.

"Nervous?" Jake asked, obviously picking up on her anxiety.

"Nervous," she admitted. "And eager. I'm really hoping in the next few minutes we'll get the answer

I need to make all this craziness stop. I need to know who is doing all this to me and why."

"That would definitely be a good thing," he replied. They broke into a small clearing, and he stopped the truck in front of a weathered wooden gate spray-painted with the words No Trespassing.

In the distance a small ramshackle cabin sat next to an outbuilding that was almost the same size. A large blackened chimney rose up from the outbuilding.

Old tires, colorful wind whirligigs and a couple of old toilets sporting arrays of flowers growing from them littered the front yard. It was hard to believe the answer to the mystery might lie in the little cabin.

They got out of the truck and approached the gate to the sound of birds singing in the trees and the rustle of animals in the nearby brush.

Jake reached out to open the gate. A gunshot sounded, and the bark on the tree near where Eva stood splintered from the force of a bullet hitting it.

"Get down," Jake yelled at her. He tackled her to the ground and threw his body over the top of hers as the scent of imminent danger filled her head.

EVA'S HEART BANGED with fear and the shock of nearly being shot. What was happening? Why had the person in the cabin nearly hit her with a bullet? Jake's body covered hers, his heart hammering almost as quickly as her own.

"You okay?" he asked softly. His eyes were as dark as night and narrowed with a sharp focus.

"I… I'm okay," she replied.

Jake rose up a bit, his gaze going toward the cabin. Eva clutched at his shoulders, afraid if he rose up any more he'd catch a bullet in his head. Why on earth had they just been shot at? What was going on now?

"Riley Kincaid," Jake yelled. "We're here to ask you some questions about your knives."

"You can't fool me," a deep, raspy voice shouted back. "You look like some of those government tax people. You got the stink of tax agents, and you ain't coming in here and messing in my business. Go away and stay off my property."

"We aren't tax agents," Jake yelled back. "We have nothing to do with the government. She is Eva Martin and I'm Jake Albright. We just need to ask you some questions about your knives."

"Albright?" There was a long pause. "Are you Justin's boy?"

Jake slowly rose to his feet and motioned for Eva to stand just behind him. Her legs were still shaky, and her heart still beat far too quickly. At least they were standing up and no bullets had followed the one that had scared her half to death.

"Yes," Jake replied. "Justin is my father."

Eva held her breath. The man with the gun might not be a fan of the Albrights. Maybe he hated them and would shoot at them again, and standing here they both made perfect targets.

Riley Kincaid stepped out onto the porch. He was a tall, thin man clad in a pair of worn jeans and a dirty white T-shirt. Frizzy gray hair fell to his shoulders, and he held a rifle in his hand. "Well, why in the hell didn't you say so in the first place? Come on in."

Jake threw his arm around her shoulders and then opened the gate. Together they advanced toward the weatherworn cabin. She released a sigh of relief as Riley leaned the gun against the porch rail.

"So, you're Jake Albright," Riley said. "Your daddy speaks well of you." He grinned, exposing a missing front tooth. "That man loves my knives."

"Unfortunately, he passed away several days ago," Jake replied.

"Well, that's a damn shame." Riley frowned and then grinned once again. "Even with all his buckets of money, he always tried to talk me down on the price of my knives. We'd haggle for an hour or so before he'd finally pay me what I wanted. Sometimes I'd knock off a couple of dollars just to make him feel better about it."

"We'd like to ask you some questions about people who have bought your knives," Jake said.

"Well, come on inside and we'll talk."

The living room/kitchen was obviously Riley's work area. Two pieces of plywood were set up like workbenches, each of them holding knife handles in various stages of completion. Wood shavings and dust covered the floor.

"Have you seen any of my knives?" he asked.

"Only one," Eva replied.

"Let me show you some of them," he said and led them to the workbench. It was obvious the man was very proud of his hand-carved handles, as he should be. The handles held the images of birds and dogs and all kinds of wildlife.

They were all absolutely exquisite, except one that instantly sent her heart racing and her hands trembling. The handle had the carving of a wolf on it. Even though it wasn't exact, the knife looked very close to the one that had been stabbed through the heart left hanging on her porch railing.

Although Eva was eager to get to the matter at hand, and despite the fear that the wolf knife brought back to her, she couldn't help but admire the obvious talent Riley had in carving something beautiful into a simple piece of wood.

"These are all so beautiful," she said.

"If you want, I can show you my setup in the outbuilding. That's where I make the blades. They're all good and balanced and very sharp," Riley said.

"Thanks, but what we really need is some answers from you," Jake said.

"Then let's sit and talk," Riley replied.

There was only a worn recliner in the work area. He led them to a small kitchen table, where they all sat. "Can I get you something to drink? Or maybe a little snack?"

"No, thank you," Eva replied. She couldn't imagine what the man would provide as a little snack. But she couldn't help but notice the cockroaches that scurried across the kitchen counters. The fact that they were active even in the daytime let her know his roach problem was huge. She definitely had no appetite to eat anything he might prepare for them.

"Thanks, but we're good," Jake said. "What we'd like to find out is if you keep records of who buys your knives."

"I've got records of who buys from me directly, but they're sold in three different stores, and once a month or so I go in and they pay me for the knives I've sold, but I don't get no names from them."

"Could we have a list of who you've sold to directly?" Jake asked. "We're especially interested in the ones that have wolf handles."

Riley narrowed his pale blue eyes. "Are you sure you're not working with the damned tax people?"

"I promise you we aren't," Eva said and then proceeded to tell him about why they were interested. She explained to him about the dead cows and then the heart hung on her porch by one of Riley's knives.

"Now that just ticks me the hell off," Riley said when she was finished. "My knives are meant to be collectibles, not to be used for such evil intent." He rose from the table and disappeared into what Eva presumed was a small bedroom.

Anxiety still fired through Eva. To her surprise Jake reached across the table and took one of her hands in his. He cast her a reassuring smile. She shouldn't have been surprised by his gesture. He'd always been able to read her mind, to read her moods.

As Riley returned carrying a spiral notebook, Jake released her hand and sat up straighter in the chair, obviously as eager as she was for any information Riley could give them.

"How far back you want me to go? I've been selling these knives in the stores and from my website for the past five years or so." He opened the notebook, which displayed surprisingly pretty and neat handwriting.

"We're really interested in the ones with wolf handles," Jake said.

Riley frowned. "I didn't keep records of what was on the knife handles, and the wolf knives are really popular."

"Then let's start with a year ago and see if any of the names you have ring a bell," Jake said.

"You tell me, girlie, if you recognize one of these people," Riley said to Eva. "I want to know who disrespected my knife by doing something so wicked to you."

Eva had never been called "girlie" in her life, and normally she'd be offended as hell by the term. But she knew Riley hadn't used it to diminish her. Besides, she was here for answers, not to get all riled up about political correctness.

"Do you know how many knives Justin Albright bought from you?" Eva asked. If Justin hadn't been sick when her whole ordeal had started, she would have suspected he was behind the attacks on her.

She would have thought that he believed Jake was getting homesick enough to return and he'd tried to drive her out of town before Jake returned home. But Justin Albright was dead and the threats were ongoing.

"I believe he bought ten in total."

Eva turned and looked at Jake. "Do you know where those knives are?"

"I don't know right now, but I'll find out before the day is over," he replied.

She knew Jake's father wasn't responsible, but maybe it was possible one of his knives had been stolen and used. She didn't want to leave any stone unturned in trying to find out who was responsible for her fear.

Riley began to read off the names of his customers. With each one he mentioned, Eva's hope that she might find an answer here began to wane. The names were unfamiliar to her.

"Griff Ainsley," Riley said, and the name caused all the hairs at the nape of her neck to rise up.

"Your high school barn partier," Jake said.

She nodded. Was it possible this was all the work of a bunch of teenagers? Could kids really be this evil? She just found it so unbelievable. Had the knife Griff bought been the same one that had stabbed through a cow's heart?

Riley continued to read off names. When he read

the name Carl Robinson, Jake frowned. "Do you know Carl?" he asked her.

"No, I don't know him. Why?"

"He works as a ranch hand for us."

"Since I don't even know him, I think it's safe to say he isn't our man," she said.

Riley continued, and another name he read off surprised her. "I know him." She straightened in the uncomfortable wooden chair. "Robert Stephenson is Bobby's dad, and Bobby is Andy's best friend."

"You ever have any issues with him?" Jake asked.

"No, on the contrary—he's always been very pleasant to me. He's mentioned several times that he'd like the boys and him and me to go out for pizza or ice cream."

"And are you interested in doing that?" Jake's eyes bored into hers.

Her face flushed with warmth. "No, I've told you I'm not interested in forming any kind of a romantic relationship with anyone."

Riley laughed and clapped his knee in glee. "I would have sworn you two were lovers. Hell, there's enough tension between you to light a fire."

Eva's cheeks warmed even more. "We're just old friends," she replied.

Riley laughed again and winked at Jake. "She might say that now, but nobody knows what the future might bring."

Jake looked at Eva, and his lips slid into his damned sexy, knowing grin. She frowned back at him. She was determined that she would never have a romantic relationship with him again.

If she had a life to live, it was one that couldn't have Jake Albright in it.

Chapter Six

"We should be able to go to the last convenience store before heading out to get you home for Andy," Jake said. He glanced over to Eva, who had fallen quiet as the frustrating day had worn on.

"If this one is like the last two we visited, it won't be any help," she replied dispiritedly.

Riley had given them the locations of the three stores that sold his knives. Unfortunately the stores hadn't kept the names of the people who had bought knives. The only way they might get any information was if somebody used a credit card for the purchase, but in that case Jake and Eva would have to have a warrant.

"Don't get discouraged," Jake said. "At least we have two more names than we did."

"I can't believe that Robert Stephenson would do all this to retaliate against me because I wouldn't go out for pizza with him and the boys," she replied dryly.

"You can never be sure what goes on in somebody else's mind. I mean, somebody killed Walter, for crying out loud. There can be all kinds of craziness, mental illness and just plain evil that people can hide from everyone."

"Jeez, that's encouraging," she said.

"We'll get him, Eva. We'll figure out who is doing this to you and we'll put his butt in jail." He could tell his words did little to assuage the depression that was slowly taking hold of her.

"Maybe I should have just sold out and left town when I received that first threatening note," she said softly.

He shot her a look of surprise. "This can't be Tom Taylor's daughter speaking right now. Tom, who loved his land and envisioned it being passed down from generation to generation."

She released a tremulous sigh. "You're right. I need to stay strong, if not for myself, then for Andy. The ranch is his legacy. It's all I have to give him. I'm just discouraged and more than a little bit tired right now."

He reached out and captured her hand with his. "Then I'll be your strength when you're tired." He released her hand. He wished they weren't in his truck but rather standing in her living room so he could pull her into his arms and hold her tight.

The third convenience store was like the other two. They could get no information from them and were told to come back with a warrant.

"At least we've done the preliminary footwork for

Wayne," Jake said as they headed home. "Let's just hope Wayne solves the murder case quickly and can focus his full attention back on this."

"We'll see if the two we know of who bought knives still have them in their possession," she said. "And I'd definitely like to be there when he talks to Griff again. That little creep has already lied to Wayne about me. I want to be there to call him out if he tries to lie again."

He shot her a quick grin. "Now that's the strong and amazing Eva I know."

She fell silent once again and stared out the window as if lost in thought. There had been a time when he could easily guess what she was thinking and feeling. But at the moment he had no clue what thoughts were whirling through her brain.

She looked so beautiful, clad in a pair of tight jeans and a sleeveless red blouse that showcased her full breasts and slender waist.

He clenched his hands tighter on the steering wheel. He wanted to get lost in the scent of her hair, to feel the silkiness of her skin against his own. There was no question he wanted her physically, but he wanted more.

He wanted every thought in her head and every dream she might entertain. He wanted her laughter and her tears, her hopes and her fears. He'd missed the last ten years of her life, but he wanted her from this time on and forever. And he wanted the person who was terrorizing her caught and thrown into a jail cell to rot.

She remained quiet until he parked back in front of her house. "I'll call Wayne and tell him what we found out," he said when they were out of the truck.

"Thanks. I'll hope to hear from him in the next couple of days, and I'll talk to you then." It was obviously a dismissal.

He looked at his watch. "It's just about time for Andy's bus to come. Mind if I hang out and say hi to him?"

He saw the hesitation in her eyes, but after a moment's pause, she said that would be fine.

They fell into step together as they walked down the lane to where the bus would stop. When they reached her mailbox at the end of the long driveway, she opened it and reached inside and grabbed a couple of envelopes.

"Any nefarious notes?" he asked once she'd flipped through all of them.

"No, just a handful of bills," she replied and frowned.

"Eva, how are you doing financially?"

Her shoulders visibly stiffened. "I really don't think that's any of your business."

"I just thought if you needed a bit of a loan or anything, I could always help out."

"I don't need or want any of your money, Jake," she protested. "I've never wanted anything to do with your money."

"I know that. I just want you to know if you ever get in a bad place, I'm always here for you," he replied. He took a step closer to her. The sun sparkled in her hair, and his head filled with the memories of making sweet, hot love with her.

She gazed up at him, and in her eyes he saw those memories were there, burning bright within her. "Eva," he murmured softly. But her eyes suddenly cooled.

"I know the Albrights have always been wealthy enough to pretty much buy whatever they wanted, but Jake, you can't buy your way back into my life," she said.

"Eva, that certainly wasn't my intention…" His protest was lost to the sound of the school bus arriving. It stopped by the drive, and the doors opened for Andy to get off. Any further talk between them was lost.

"Mr. Jake." Andy greeted him with a wide smile. "Are we going fishing again today?"

"Not today." Jake grinned and ruffled the boy's dark hair. "But we'll plan to go again real soon."

"You want to come in and have a snack with me? Mom usually makes me a snack before I start doing my homework. Maybe if you stay, Mom will give us cookies instead of dumb old carrot and celery sticks."

Eva laughed. "Carrot and celery sticks are good for you."

"Yeah, but cookies are just good," Andy quipped back.

Eva and Jake both laughed. "How was school?" Jake asked as they headed back toward the house. He was concerned about how Eva had taken his offer to help her. He'd certainly not intended for her to think he was trying to somehow buy her, but this was a subject for them to discuss at another time.

"It was good." As Andy talked about his day, a warmth rushed through Jake. This was what life was all about…walking children home from school… listening to them share their days and smiling over their heads at the woman you loved.

He wanted this, not just for now, but for forever. He could easily love Andy, who had no father and was a part of Eva. He wanted to make more babies with her and build a life with her.

However, first he had to make her want that same thing with him. The only thing she was offering him at the moment was cookies and milk.

Patience, he told himself. He had to be patient even though he wanted all of her now. His chest tightened as he thought of everything that had happened.

The most important thing right now was making sure they got the perpetrator who was tormenting her behind bars. That needed to happen before the creep got a chance to hurt or kill Eva.

Leaving the heart on her front porch was definitely an escalation. What concerned Jake the most was if the person escalated even more, there was no way to guess what he might do next.

THE NEXT MORNING Eva waved goodbye to Andy as the school bus whisked him away. The heat had abated somewhat overnight, but a stiff wind blew, screaming around the sides of the buildings and driving Eva just a little bit crazy.

She walked back to the house, but before she got inside, Wayne's official car turned into her drive, followed by Jake's pickup.

Jake. He'd been on her mind all night. He'd even occupied a prominent role in her dreams...dreams that were filled with passion and desire and the memories of what once had been between them.

Watching him interact with Andy made her want things she couldn't have. She wanted Jake, but she could never, would never have any kind of a future with him.

All she wanted right now was answers, and hopefully Wayne had brought some with him. She was surprised to see him, since he and his men had a murder case to solve. She watched as the two vehicles parked and the men got out.

"Morning, Eva," Wayne said in greeting. "I hope you have the coffee on."

"As a matter of fact, I do." She nodded to Jake and then opened the front door to allow them in. "Wayne, I didn't expect to see you so soon. What about Walter's murder case? I thought you were all tied up with that." She poured them all a cup of coffee and then joined them at the table.

"The murder has been solved. Sadie confessed to it late last night," Wayne replied.

Eva gasped in stunned surprise. "What? Sadie

killed her husband? My God, is this some kind of a joke?" She couldn't imagine the sweet old lady hurting a fly.

Wayne nodded. "No joke. She said she was sick of him bossing her around, and she was disgusted by his snoring every night and her not being able to enjoy the master bedroom. She hated the way his dentures clicked and how his ears were so hairy and he refused to let the barber clean them up." Wayne shrugged. "She said she just snapped. She got up in the middle of the night, grabbed a knife and stabbed him."

"I would never have guessed that Sadie was capable of such a violent thing," Eva replied.

"Oh, we were pretty sure it was Sadie right from the get-go," Wayne said. "Mainly because there were no signs of forced entry and the knife she used was right from the kitchen countertop. It was just a matter of time before she finally confessed that she'd done it."

He took a long swig from his coffee cup, and then continued, "Anyway, Jake has caught me up on what you two found out yesterday from Riley Kincaid, and he mentioned that you'd like to come along when I question Griff once again."

"Definitely," Eva said forcefully. "Just thinking about the lies that kid has already told about me makes my blood boil."

"If I take you along for the interview, you'll have to keep your temper in check," Wayne warned her with a frown.

"Oh, don't worry, I promise I'll behave," she replied. "So when are you going to go talk to him again?"

"As soon as I have another cup of your coffee," Wayne replied.

She frowned. "Isn't he in school right now? Don't you have to wait and question him with his parents in attendance?"

"Actually, since last time he interviewed the kid, Wayne learned a very interesting fact," Jake said. "Griff is eighteen years old. He's legally an adult."

"And so that means I can question him all I like until he asks for a lawyer. Now…about that second cup of coffee?"

Eva poured him another cup. "What about the convenience stores that sell the knives?"

"I'll be writing up warrants tonight and taking them to Judge Himes first thing in the morning. At least we should be able to take a look at credit card transactions and get the names of all the people who bought those knives on credit. Unfortunately there's no way we can know the names of anyone who paid cash in the stores."

"And what about Robert Stephenson? I'm sure you're intending to talk to him as well," Jake said.

"Sure, but Robert is an upstanding man in the community. Besides owning a successful insurance agency, he's also on the town council," Wayne said. "I just can't imagine him having any part in this."

"And Sadie was just a sweet old woman," Jake said dryly.

"Point taken." Wayne drained his coffee and then stood. "So, are we ready to take a trip to the high school?"

"Just let me grab my purse," Eva said.

"If you want, Eva, you can ride with me," Jake offered. "As I remember, parking was always difficult at the high school. Of course, the last time I parked there was ten years ago."

"Nothing much has changed in the last ten years," Wayne replied. "It's still hard to find open parking spaces because so many of the students drive to school."

Minutes later Eva was in Jake's truck, an followed Wayne's patrol car into town junior high and high school buildin just off Main Street. Andy's gra opposite end of Main.

Like Jake, Eva hadn' for the past ten yea cafeteria food she was s nearl

h head her clas he'd have own class.

After he gr they'd planned i

for stolen kisses and sweet-talk with her during the days. It had been the happiest time in her entire life.

As they stood in the office waiting for Griff to be brought in, she hazarded a glance at Jake. She was shocked to see him staring at her with the heat of yesteryear burning bright in his eyes.

Would they have made it together if his father hadn't interfered? Would they have really gotten married and lived happily ever after? There was no way to know now. She forced her gaze away from him.

At that moment Griff swaggered into the office and pulled himself up short at the sight of the three of them waiting for him.

"Hey, what's going on here?" he asked indignantly. "What's she doing here?" He narrowed his brown eyes as he gazed at Eva.

"Mrs. Pritchard, would it be possible for us to the privacy of your office for a little while?" e asked.

course." The school principal led them to e room with a large desk and six chairs wall.

ickly rearranged the chairs so Griff sat e adults. Griff was a big, good-looking lond hair and a confident air that Eva im very popular with the girls and boys.

?" he asked the moment Wayne

closed the door and then turned to face him. "Why do you want to talk to me again?"

"We just have a few more questions for you, Griff," Wayne said.

"You already asked me questions, and I can tell you I got no more answers for you."

He smirked, and Eva wanted to pinch his impertinent head off his sturdy neck. It was obvious Griff had little respect for Wayne or the other two adults in the room.

"We understand you bought a knife from Riley Kincaid about six months ago," Wayne said.

The smirk on Griff's face quickly disappeared. "Yeah, so what? That's not against the law."

"They are fine-looking knives," Jake said.

"And who are you?" Griff asked.

"My name is Jake Albright."

Griff's eyes darkened. "Albright...why are you here? What do you have to do with anything?"

"I'm here because Eva is a close friend of mine and I understand you like to party in her barn uninvited," Jake replied. There was a steely strength in his tone.

"I don't know what you're talking about," Griff replied and looked down at his feet.

"We both know that isn't true," Eva said evenly.

"What kind of animal was on your Kincaid knife?" Wayne asked.

Griff frowned. "I don't know... I think it was a wolf or a leopard."

'Which was it?" Jake asked. "A wolf or a leopard?"

"I said I don't remember." Griff's tone held obvious irritation.

"Where's your knife now, Griff?" Wayne asked.

Griff looked at Wayne in surprise. "My knife? Uh… I don't know where it is. I lost it somewhere."

Wayne frowned. "When, exactly, did you lose it?"

Griff shrugged. "I don't know, a couple of months ago. What's the big deal?"

"The big deal is somebody stabbed a cow's heart into my porch railing using one of Kincaid's knives," Eva said.

Griff's eyes widened and then narrowed. "I have nothing to do with that," he exclaimed. "A cow's heart? That's totally disgusting."

"Then where is your knife?" Eva asked. "It's very coincidental that you don't have the knife you bought and Wayne now has one in evidence. Too bad you don't remember where you lost it."

"I did lose it." Griff looked frantically at Jake and then at Wayne. His cheeks grew red. "Okay, some of us sometimes have had parties in her barn. The last time I remember having the knife was at one of the parties, and when I got home I realized it was gone."

"So, you think your knife is someplace in Eva's barn?" Jake asked.

"I think so," Griff replied. He shifted in his chair, obviously uncomfortable. "Can I go back to class now? I had nothing to do with stabbing a cow's heart.

"Point taken." Wayne drained his coffee and then stood. "So, are we ready to take a trip to the high school?"

"Just let me grab my purse," Eva said.

"If you want, Eva, you can ride with me," Jake offered. "As I remember, parking was always difficult at the high school. Of course, the last time I parked there was ten years ago."

"Nothing much has changed in the last ten years," Wayne replied. "It's still hard to find open parking spaces because so many of the students drive to school."

Minutes later Eva was in Jake's truck, and they followed Wayne's patrol car into town, where the junior high and high school buildings were located just off Main Street. Andy's grade school was on the opposite end of Main.

Like Jake, Eva hadn't been back to the high school for the past ten years. Walking inside to the smell of cafeteria food and the faint odor of the locker rooms, she was struck with a wave of nostalgia so strong it nearly weakened her knees.

It had been within these walls that she had fallen head over heels in love with Jake. He'd walk her to her classes, and they'd talk until the bell rang and he'd have to hurry off before he was tardy for his own class.

After he graduated, when she was still a senior, they'd planned it so he could sneak in a back door for stolen kisses and sweet-talk with her during the days. It had been the happiest time in her entire life.

As they stood in the office waiting for Griff to be brought in, she hazarded a glance at Jake. She was shocked to see him staring at her with the heat of yesteryear burning bright in his eyes.

Would they have made it together if his father hadn't interfered? Would they have really gotten married and lived happily ever after? There was no way to know now. She forced her gaze away from him.

At that moment Griff swaggered into the office and pulled himself up short at the sight of the three of them waiting for him.

"Hey, what's going on here?" he asked indignantly. "What's she doing here?" He narrowed his brown eyes as he gazed at Eva.

"Mrs. Pritchard, would it be possible for us to use the privacy of your office for a little while?" Wayne asked.

"Of course." The school principal led them to a nice-size room with a large desk and six chairs against the wall.

Wayne quickly rearranged the chairs so Griff sat facing the three adults. Griff was a big, good-looking guy with short blond hair and a confident air that Eva was sure made him very popular with the girls and a leader among the boys.

"What's going on?" he asked the moment Wayne

That's messed up, and I swear I don't know anything about that."

Wayne looked at Jake and Eva and then back at Griff. "We may be back with more questions, Griff."

Eva stood. "And stay the hell out of my barn."

"What do you think?" Wayne asked a few minutes later when they were outside the school.

"I think he's a sly little creep," Jake replied.

"Do you think he was telling the truth about the knife?" Wayne asked.

"I don't know what to believe, but if that knife is in my barn, I'll find it," Eva said.

"Eva and I can both search the barn so you can work on getting the warrants ready for the convenience stores. You'll stay in touch?" Jake asked.

"Of course," Wayne replied. "And you let me know right away if you find that knife."

He returned to his patrol car, and Jake and Eva got back into the truck. "If Andy ever shows evidence that he's turning into a Griff, I'll lock him in his room for the rest of his life," she said.

Jake laughed. "Trust me, Andy doesn't have an ounce of Griff in him, because he has a mama who is raising him with the right morals and values."

"I hope so," she replied. "I sometimes worry that I'm being too hard on Andy, and then I worry that I'm being too soft on him."

"I think that's normal," Jake replied with a small laugh. "You are an amazing mother, Eva."

"Thanks." She stared out the window. And Jake

would be an amazing father. But it was too late for that. If he discovered now that Andy was his son, he would hate her for the years lost. And in his hatred, with his power and money, he could take Andy away from her forever.

Chapter Seven

Eva's barn held the horses' stalls and square bales of hay stacked in the back and hundreds of memories that immediately assailed Jake when they walked inside.

She led him to the back of the barn. "This is where I usually find the most trash after one of their parties," she said. "If Griff lost his knife in here, then it's either in this area or upstairs in the loft. I usually find trash up there, too."

He looked around the hay-covered floor and then back at her. "Then we'll start our search here." He grabbed a pitchfork from the corner and began to move the hay on the earthen floor to one side. She got a lawn rake and began to do the same.

He tried to focus on the task at hand, but he couldn't stop the memories that rushed through his brain. It had been here, in this general area, that he and Eva had given their virginities to each other.

That night she had sneaked out of the house with a blanket to meet him in the barn. He'd brought a kerosene lantern that had provided a cozy glow. It had been a night of sweet exploration and discovery and had led to many more passionate trysts in the barn.

They now worked together, the only sound in the barn their tools scraping against the floor. He shot her several surreptitious looks, wondering if she was thinking about their past lovemaking, too.

It was impossible to tell what she was thinking at the moment. Her face was devoid of any expression, and she swept the hay with swift, almost angry strokes.

It didn't take long for them to clear the hay from one area and then sweep it back where it belonged. She frowned and leaned against the rake handle.

"This is like literally hunting for a needle in a haystack," she said in obvious frustration. "And we don't even know if Griff was telling the truth about losing the knife in here. For all we know, it was his knife stabbed through that heart."

"You're right, but we need to check in case he was telling the truth. Let's take a quick look around the loft and then we can call it a day," he suggested.

She nodded, and a moment later he followed her up the ladder to the loft. Up here there were more stacks of hay. This area also held a wealth of memories.

It was here that he and she had conducted their very own solemn mock marriage ceremony. They had pledged their hearts and souls to each other, vowing to make the marriage real as soon as she graduated from high school in two months' time.

He looked at her now, with the heat of his thoughts burning inside him. At the same time, her gaze met his. For a moment time seemed to stand still.

He slowly leaned his pitchfork against a stack of hay and took a step toward her...and then another. She didn't back away from him, and that's when he knew she was caught up in the memories as well.

"Eva," he said softly. He reached out and took the rake from her hand and leaned it against another bale of hay. She stood as still as a beautiful statue.

"Sweet Eva." He reached out and dragged his fingers down the side of her face. She closed her eyes and turned into his caress, giving him the courage to gather her into his arms.

"Do you remember, Eva?" he whispered softly into her ear. "Do you remember how it was between us?"

She opened her eyes, and her lips parted in invitation. That's all he needed. He covered her mouth with his as his arms tightened around her.

Immediately he was half-crazy with the smell of her, with the feel of her soft breasts against his chest and the length of her legs along his own.

Her mouth opened wider to allow his tongue entry, and he took full advantage, swirling his with hers as his pulse accelerated. She was hot in his blood. She always had been, and nothing had changed.

She leaned into him, and one of her arms crept

up so her fingers could toy with the hair at the nape of his neck. He moved his lips down the side of her jaw, and she leaned her head back to give him full access to her throat.

Tangling his hands in her thick, silken hair, he couldn't hold back the groan of desire that escaped him. His body had spent the last ten years missing hers, and now to have her back in his arms was beyond wonderful.

"Tell me that you've thought about this…about us over the years," he said. He leaned back slightly so he could see her features.

Her eyes were the deepest violet of dusk and shone with a hunger that nearly stole his breath away. "Yes…yes, I've thought about this." Her voice was barely audible, as if she was reluctantly admitting to a sin.

She stared at him for another long moment, and then she pushed away from him and stepped back. "But I'm not sixteen years old anymore, and I'm not about to have sex in a hayloft with a man who walked out on me ten years ago."

Desire was replaced with stunned surprise. "I didn't walk out on you, Eva. You pushed me out. You told me you were through with me, that you didn't love me anymore."

Her cheeks flushed with color. "Well, you certainly didn't stick around to fight for my love. As I remember, the next day you were on a plane to Italy, and you never looked back."

He raked a hand through his hair and frowned. "Eva, you gutted me that night. I couldn't even think straight. You pulled the rug out from under my life and the future I thought we'd have together."

He paused a moment, his breath caught in his chest as old, painful emotions threatened to overwhelm him. "Eva, did you really think I was going to just hang around here and watch you date other guys? I would have gone totally insane."

For a long moment, their gazes remained locked, and then she looked away and released a tremulous sigh. "I'm sorry about the way things worked out between us, Jake. But we were both so young."

She sighed again and then grabbed both the pitchfork and rake in her hand. "I'm done. Let's get out of here."

He took the tools from her and followed her down the ladder. Once again he leaned the pitchfork and rake in the corner and then turned to look at her.

"Eva, I never stopped loving you."

"Jake, you were in love with a young teenage girl. I'm not that girl anymore." Her gaze drifted to a place just over his head. "You need to get over the past. Jake, I'm never going to fall in love again. I have no intention of ever marrying again." Her gaze met his once again. "Don't love me, Jake. It's a total waste of your time."

She walked out of the barn, and he slowly followed behind her. He wished it were that easy, that he could just shut off all his emotions where she was concerned.

Had her marriage been so bad that she never wanted to marry again? Or had her marriage been so good she didn't want to try again with anyone else? Were her memories of loving her husband enough to keep her happy for the rest of her life?

"Eva, you can't deny that there's still something between us," he finally said.

"Lust," she replied tersely. "I won't deny that there is a strong physical attraction between us, but that's all it is, and it's something I certainly don't intend to explore."

"That's not the message you were sending to me a few minutes ago," he replied.

Her cheeks flushed a deep pink once again. "And that won't happen again. Jake, I've moved on. I've got enough chaos in my life right now, and I don't need any more."

"I'm sorry, Eva. The last thing I want to do is make your life more difficult." A bit of guilt swept through him. She was right. She had a crazy person after her, and he had been just thinking about his own wants and needs. Totally selfish on his part.

"Let's just move on." She looked away from him again. "And now I've got things to do before Andy gets home from school."

"You'll let me know if you hear anything from Wayne?"

"Of course I will," she replied.

Jake got in his truck and headed home. He'd been foolish to believe that Eva would be open to having a relationship with him right now.

She had a crazy person killing her cattle and making threats on her life. She had no idea who might be a danger to her and how that danger might play itself out.

He was sure she was in no state of mind to think about romance or relationships right now, and he'd been a selfish fool to express his feelings for her at this point in time.

Still, he couldn't imagine that a beautiful, vibrant twenty-eight-year-old woman would completely close herself off from love for the rest of her life. Eventually Andy was going to grow up and move on with his life, and he couldn't imagine Eva would want to be all alone forever.

He'd wait and hope that the perp was caught soon, and then all bets were off and he intended to pursue Eva and make her see that they were really meant to be together forever.

"WE HAD A portion of the fence down on the west side of the pasture this morning," Harley said to Eva.

Jake had left minutes before, and Harley had appeared at the kitchen door. She now sat facing him across the kitchen table. "How did that happen?" she asked.

"Looked to me like it was intentionally pulled down. Thankfully no cattle got out, the fence wasn't damaged and Jimmy and I were able to get it back up."

Eva released a deep sigh. "I swear, if it's not one thing, then it's another."

"At least there were no dead cows this morning," Harley replied. "I can deal with a downed fence."

"Thank goodness for small favors," Eva replied dryly.

"Any news from Wayne on solving this whole mess?"

"Not much, but I have to admit he's working hard on it. Of course he got thrown off for a day with Walter's murder."

Harley frowned. "Hell of a thing, wasn't it? Who would believe that Sadie had that kind of rage pent up inside her? I guess you just never know about people."

"I still find it hard to believe," Eva replied.

"At least it was a quick solve for Wayne."

"Yeah, he said he knew it was Sadie from the very beginning. It was just a matter of how long it was going to take her to confess."

"On a happier note, the herd is looking really good. All of them are nice and healthy."

She flashed a smile to Harley. "Thanks for a bit of good news for a change."

Harley stood. "Well, I just wanted to let you know about the fence. Jimmy and I intend to ride the fence line at dusk tonight to make sure there are no more problems, and we'll check it all again around dawn."

"That's going above and beyond," Eva replied. Neither Jimmy nor Harley lived on Eva's property, and their chores were usually done by five or six in the evening, and they went to their homes. If they intended to be here until dusk tonight, that meant they would be working late.

"We don't mind. We both want to do what we can to help you. We understand these are unusual circumstances. Hopefully Wayne will make the arrests that need to be made in this case and things will get back to normal around here."

Eva got up and walked with him to the back door. "I've almost forgotten what normal is around here."

"Keep your chin up, Eva. You'll get through all this," Harley said with a reassuring smile. "You're as tough as they come."

"Thanks, Harley."

When Harley left, Eva got busy with the daily chores. She tried desperately not to think about what had happened between her and Jake earlier in the barn.

She couldn't allow anything like that to ever happen again. Her desire for Jake was definitely her weakness, and it was a weakness she couldn't afford.

There was a part of her that knew she was being unfair in wanting him to help and support her through the darkness and uncertainty of the danger she found herself in and not wanting any of his other emotions involved.

However, fair or unfair, that was exactly what she wanted and needed from him. She hadn't realized until now how truly isolated she'd become from any other people who might support her through this ordeal. Other than her two ranch hands, she really had nobody else in her life.

Until now...until Jake.

She'd been so busy working to survive, working to keep her ranch so her son would have something for himself when he got older, that she hadn't made any real adult friendships.

When this was all over, maybe it was time she tried to rectify that. There had been times in the past when one of Andy's friends' mothers had invited her for coffee or a quick lunch at the café or drinks in the evening, but Eva had always declined those invitations, telling herself she didn't have time for socializing. And yet she couldn't regret that she'd spent every spare moment when she wasn't working around the ranch with her son.

At least she'd made it clear to Jake that he had no future with her. If he wanted to continue to support her through everything, then he was forewarned that there was nothing else in it for him.

By the time Andy got off the school bus, she'd successfully put all crazy thoughts of Jake, and any other negative thoughts, out of her head. It was impossible to sustain the simmer of fear every minute of every hour of every day. If she allowed her fear to completely consume her, then she'd go mad.

"We have to do the egg deliveries tonight, Mom," Andy said as they walked back to the house from the bus stop.

"I know. All you need to do is package up the eggs and I'll drive you...unless you'd rather me package up all the eggs and you drive me."

Andy laughed. "Mom, you're a silly goofball. You know I can't drive."

"Oh, that's right. I forgot for a minute." As always Andy's laughter warmed her heart. "We'll eat dinner and then head out. In the meantime, you get the deliveries ready to go while I get the meal on the table."

It was just after five thirty when she and Andy got into her pickup to make the rounds of the deliveries. They had six houses to go to this evening, and then Saturday they would make deliveries to half a dozen more people.

Eva didn't give her son an allowance. Instead he earned his money with his egg business. He fed the chickens in the mornings, cleaned out their coops, gathered eggs and then he sold them. She took a percentage of the money he made to buy cartons and feed so he would learn that there was a cost to profit. He had a little record book and was diligent in writing in it after each delivery date. She considered the process a teaching tool, and he was proud of earning the money he got to spend.

She watched him now as he returned to the truck after making his final delivery of the night. "Mrs. Edwards wants four dozen eggs next week instead of two," he said with excitement. "She said she's got family visiting and they all love her deviled eggs."

"That means a little more money in your pocket

next week," Eva replied. "Can I tell you a little secret?"

"Yeah, what secret?" Andy looked at her curiously.

"Mrs. Edwards makes the worst deviled eggs I've ever tasted," Eva said.

Andy giggled. "Really?"

"Really. She brought them to the little buffet we all put together after the last school fair, and they were yucky."

Andy giggled again. "At least she's buying extra eggs next week. I was thinking maybe we could celebrate by getting ice cream on the way home," Andy said. "I'll treat you with my own money."

"Hmm, that sounds like an offer I can't resist."

Minutes later they were seated in the ice cream shop with sundaes before them. "Mom, can I ask you a question?" Andy swirled his spoon through his hot fudge.

"You can always ask me anything," she replied.

"When did you know Mr. Jake before?"

"What do you mean?" she asked, not sure she understood.

"He said he was an old friend of yours, but I never saw him before."

"He was my best friend when I was in high school," she replied.

"So, what happened? Why didn't you stay best friends?"

"He went away for work, and then I got married to

your daddy and Jake and I just lost touch with each other. Why all the questions?"

"I was just wondering," Andy replied. "I like Mr. Jake a lot. He was so nice to me when we went fishing together."

She wanted to tell her son not to get too attached to Jake, that ultimately he wouldn't be in their lives for long. But of course she didn't say any of that.

In any case, before she could reply, the door to the ice cream parlor swung open and Robert Stephenson and Bobby came in.

Bobby rushed over to where they sat, and the two boys high-fived each other in greeting. "We were just walking by and saw the two of you in here," Robert said. "Mind if we join you?"

"Not at all," Eva replied, although she felt slightly uncomfortable knowing that Robert was on the list of people who had bought a knife from Riley Kincaid. She had no idea if Wayne had spoken to him about it yet or not.

Robert and Bobby got their ice cream and then settled at the table with Eva and Andy. As the boys chattered together, Robert smiled at Eva. "You look really pretty tonight, Eva. Red is definitely a good color for you."

"Thank you," she replied, even more uncomfortable beneath his intense gaze.

Thankfully Andy and Bobby began speaking with the adults about plans for a sleepover the next weekend. Even though it was Eva's turn to have the boys at her house, Bobby wanted Andy to stay at their home because the two boys had a big puzzle they were working on together that wouldn't transport to Eva's place.

By the time the arrangements had been made, Eva and Andy were finished with their ice cream. "It was nice seeing you, Robert," Eva said as she and Andy got up from the table.

"It's always a pleasure to see you, Eva," he replied.

"Bobby's dad likes you," Andy said when they were back in the truck and heading home. "Bobby told me his dad wants to take you out on a date. If you two got married, then Bobby and I would be brothers."

"Whoa, that's not going to happen," Eva replied. "Bobby's dad seems like a very nice man, but I'm not going to go out on a date with him, and I'm definitely not going to marry him."

"Maybe you could marry Mr. Jake instead. Then he'd be my dad. That would be so cool. I know you like him and he likes you, and I really, really like him."

Eva's heart squeezed tight. "Andy, I can't just marry somebody to give you a dad. There's a lot more to a marriage than that."

"Okay, if I can't have a dad, then could we get a puppy?" He looked at her appealingly.

Eva laughed with more than a little bit of relief.

"Now, that's something we can definitely think about."

An hour later Andy was tucked into bed and Eva wandered the house restlessly. It had been a long day, but she wasn't even close to being ready for bed.

She finally grabbed a house key and a cell phone she kept for Andy. She crept into his bedroom and placed the phone on his nightstand. She stood for a long moment just watching him sleep.

She had fallen in love for a second time in her life the moment Andy had been placed in her arms after birth. He'd been a beautiful, good baby who rarely fussed. His presence in the house had brought great joy to a dying man.

Despite being sick, Andrew had tried to be a present father who had played with Andy and had often read bedtime stories to him. He'd helped Eva with the nighttime feedings and had been thrilled when Andy's first word had been *dada.*

The questions Andy had asked about her getting married again so he could have a dad had broken her heart, but that was the one thing she couldn't give him.

Turning away, she left the room and made sure she had her own phone in her pocket. She locked up the house and stepped outside.

The warm night air wrapped around her, and the sky was filled with a million stars. It wasn't unusual for her to leave the house at this time in the evening to check on the horses or finish up some chore or another. If Andy awakened, he knew where she was, and he had the phone to call her.

Tonight not only did she want to give her horses a treat, but she also wanted to spend some more time finishing checking the loft for Griff's knife. If it was up there, she was determined to find it. She just didn't know if Griff had been telling the truth about it or not.

At least she wasn't worried about Griff and his friends showing up unexpectedly to party in the barn—not with Griff knowing Wayne had him in his sights.

She opened the barn door and flipped on the light switch. Nothing happened. "Damn," she muttered beneath her breath. Apparently the lightbulb had burned out, and that particular bulb was a real pain in the neck to replace.

Because the bulb burned out on a fairly regular basis, she kept a flashlight hanging from a hook on the wall just beneath the light switch.

She grabbed the flashlight and flicked it on, shooting a path of illumination ahead of her. She didn't intend to change the bulb tonight, and that canceled out her plan to do any further search for the knife in the loft. But she could still feed the horses some treats before heading back to the house.

The horses seemed restless, sidestepping in their stalls, and as she drew closer to them, she caught a whiff of something that had no business being in a barn. It was the smell of gasoline.

Her stomach clenched, and her adrenaline shot up. She guided the light all around the area in an attempt to find the source. She took another couple of steps forward and then screamed as a dark figure lunged out of the darkness toward her.

The person wore a ski mask and had a pitchfork in his hands. "Wh-who are you? Wh-what do you want?" she asked, her heart nearly exploding in her chest. Her entire body went cold with a deep terror she'd never felt before.

He didn't answer. He stood before her for a long moment and then rushed forward and stabbed the pitchfork at her. She screamed and stumbled backward in an attempt to get away from him. He continued to advance on her, and with a sob of terror she turned to run.

Nobody knew she was out here, and there was nobody to hear her frantic cries for help. *Die, bitch.* The words on the note screamed over and over again in her head.

The flashlight slid from her hand, hit the floor and immediately went out. She headed toward the door in the distance as fast as she could, aware that he was right behind her. Sheer horror ripped through her. Her breaths escaped her on painful gasps.

He was going to kill her. There was no question in her mind that his intent was to murder her. If he caught her, he was going to use the pitchfork to take her life in a painful, horrid way. In her frantic desire to escape…she tripped.

She slid across the floor on her stomach, all the while struggling to get back up on her feet. She looked behind her just in time to see the pitchfork tines coming down. With another scream, she rolled, and the sharp tines thudded into the floor right next to her body.

As her attacker yanked at the pitchfork, she made it to her feet. However, before she could completely get away, the attacker hit her with the tines in her lower leg, piercing her with excruciating pain.

She hit the floor on her hands and knees. She scrabbled forward, sobbing and terrified that the pitchfork would strike her again, this time in the back. Instead, nothing happened. Rolling over on her back, she realized her attacker was gone.

"Mrs. Eva?"

The familiar voice came out of the darkness by the barn door. "Oh my God…what happened? Mrs. Eva…are you okay?"

"Jimmy? Jimmy, is that you?" Sobs escaped her, sobs of both pain and relief.

"It's me, Mrs. Eva." He ran to her side and crouched down next to her.

"Please…help me up," she cried. Had the attacker heard Jimmy's approach and run off? Or was he still hiding out somewhere in the barn? "Please, Jimmy, get me out of here right now."

She could scarcely think straight. "Did you see him? H-he was in the barn, and he attacked me with the pitchfork."

"I'm sorry, I didn't see anyone," Jimmy replied. "I just heard you scream, and I knew something was wrong."

Fear still torched through her, along with the pain in her leg. Jimmy helped her to her feet and slowly walked with her to the house.

Tears half blinded her as she fumbled to unlock the front door. When it opened she almost fell inside. "You're hurt," Jimmy exclaimed, as if noticing the blood on her pants leg for the first time. "What can I do to help?"

"Call Wayne," she managed to gasp through her tears. "And check out the barn. I thought I smelled gasoline in there. But be careful. Whoever attacked me might still be there."

"Don't worry about me, Mrs. Eva. If anyone is out there, I'll shoot the bastard first." Jimmy pulled his gun from his holster. "Are you sure you don't want me to stay here with you?"

"No, I'll be fine until Wayne gets here." With her thoughts still so jumbled in fear, she didn't want anyone in the house with her unless it was Wayne. She couldn't believe what had just happened to her.

Once Jimmy stepped back outside, she locked the door behind him and hobbled into her bedroom. She got her shotgun from the gun case and then returned to the living room. Tears of pain, of fear, still coursed down her cheeks.

She felt as if she was trapped in a nightmare or had entered some kind of horrible twilight zone. She couldn't believe somebody had attacked her. She turned her leg to try to look at her wounds.

"Mom?" Andy appeared in the living room doorway.

She quickly swiped at her cheeks. "Go back to bed, Andy."

"But Mom, you're bleeding." His eyes were wide and alarmed as he looked first at the blood on her jeans leg and then at the gun she had leaning up next to her. "What's happening? Mom, what's going on?"

"Honey, what I need for you to do right now is go back to your room. I'm okay, and everything is going to be fine." Dear God, she didn't want her son to see her this way. "The sheriff is coming to talk to me, and I need you to go back to your room and close the door and go to sleep."

Andy eyed her worriedly for another long moment and then did what he was told and went back to his room.

She needed to clean up her leg, but at the moment she couldn't move as an icy chill filled her heart and soul. She still felt as if she were in a nightmare. But unfortunately this wasn't a dream. It was reality, and the truth of the matter was somebody had just tried to kill her.

Chapter Eight

Jake poured himself a shot of scotch from the mini-bar and then sank down on the sofa in his suite. He grabbed the remote and turned on his television. To-night he needed a distraction from his thoughts. It had been a long, emotional day, and even now he couldn't seem to shrug off thoughts of Eva. He was hoping a silly sitcom would empty his mind or at least make him sleepy.

He'd just found what he intended to watch when his cell phone rang and Eva's name came up on the caller identification. Why would she be calling him? Maybe she'd heard some news from Wayne?

"Eva?" he answered.

"No, it's me. It's Andy. Mr. Jake, my mom is bleeding on her leg and she's crying. Maybe could you come over here?"

The boy's voice shook with obvious fear, and his words shot an equal amount of apprehension through Jake. "I'm on my way, Andy. I'll be there as quick as I can."

"Okay," Andy replied with obvious relief. "Thanks, Mr. Jake."

Minutes later Jake was in his truck and driving as fast as possible to Eva's ranch. She was bleeding? Had she somehow cut herself? Jake should have asked Andy more questions, like where she was bleeding from? What had happened to her? How badly was she hurt?

He stepped on the accelerator to go even faster, grateful that there was little traffic to get in his way. His heart beat a frantic rhythm. Why hadn't Eva called him herself? Was she too incapacitated to make a phone call?

What in the hell had happened?

It seemed like it took him forever, but he finally pulled up in front of her place, cut his engine and jumped out of his truck. He raced to the door and banged on it. "Eva…Andy, it's me. Open the door."

After a long moment, the door opened and Eva collapsed into his arms. He held her tight as she sobbed into the crook of his neck. Thank God she wasn't hurt so badly that she hadn't been able to get to the door and into his arms. But she was obviously hurt, because she was weeping and clinging to him.

He let her cry for a few minutes and then pulled her arms from around his neck, leaned back and looked at her. "Eva, what happened?" he finally asked. Her eyes were dark with unmistakable fear.

He led her to the sofa, and it was then he saw the blood on the back of the lower leg of her jeans and the shotgun leaned against the corner of the couch. "You're bleeding. Honey, what happened?" he repeated.

"Wh-what are you doing here?" She spoke between barely suppressed sobs.

"Andy called me. He sounded scared and he told me you were bleeding and crying. What happened to your leg?"

"I was attacked by a man with a pitchfork in the barn and I…I think…no, I know he…he meant to kill me." She began to cry once again.

Between her tears, she told him what had happened from the time she had entered the barn to when Jimmy had helped her back to the house. When she was finished, a rich rage coupled with a chilling fear lodged in his chest.

"Let's take a look at your leg," he said. At least she was able to walk.

He knelt down in front of her, and he rolled up her jeans leg so he could get a look at the puncture wounds. There were two, but thankfully they had mostly stopped bleeding. "Maybe we should get you to the hospital to get these checked out."

"No, that's not necessary," she protested. "They hurt, but I don't think they're as deep as I originally thought. I was scurrying across the barn floor as fast as I could, and so I guess he only got a quick, glancing jab into me."

The vision her words created in his head once

again filled him with a deep anger. Dammit, who was this person and why would he want to hurt Eva?

"Let me get a warm cloth so we can clean you up. Do you have some antibiotic cream?"

"There's a medical kit in the hall closet, and there's some antibiotic cream in it," she replied.

He stood, but before he could walk to the hall closet to get a cloth, Wayne showed up.

Jake let the lawman into the house, and while he began to question Eva, Jake got the washcloth and the medical tin box and then sat next to Eva to wipe the blood off the wounds and get some antibiotic cream on them.

As she recounted to Wayne what had happened in the barn, his fear for her once again tightened his chest. "Did you get a look at the person?" Wayne asked. "Anything that might help identify him or her?"

"I'm pretty sure it was a male by the brief view I had of his size. But he wore a ski mask, and I couldn't begin to identify who he was. The barn was dark, and I only had a minute before I lost the flashlight."

Jake finished tending to her leg and then returned to sit beside her. "I was so stupid," Eva said angrily. "With everything that's been going on, I should have never gone out to the barn by myself after dark. When the light didn't work, I should have immediately turned around and run to the house."

"Can you tell me anything else about the attack or your attacker?" Wayne asked.

"It all just happened so fast." She raised a hand

to her temple and rubbed it as if trying to alleviate a headache. "He seemed to come out of nowhere. Other than believing it was a male, I can't think of anything else. I'm sorry. I… I was just so afraid."

"It's all right, Eva…take your time," Jake said. All he really wanted to do was draw her back into his arms once again until he knew there was no more danger to her and no more fear inside her.

"I really believe he would have killed me if Jimmy hadn't shown up when he did," she replied. "I sensed a hatred coming from him. At one point if I hadn't rolled away in time, the pitchfork would have struck me in my back. Why does somebody hate me enough to kill me?"

Jake frowned. "What was Jimmy doing out around there at this time of night?"

"I… I don't know," Eva replied with a frown of her own. "Harley told me earlier that he and Jimmy were going to check the fence line around dusk, but dusk was a long time ago."

"Where's Jimmy now?" Wayne asked.

"I sent him back to the barn. Right before the attack, I thought I smelled gasoline."

"Gasoline?" Another alarm shot off in Jake. It would take very little to set a fire that would destroy not only the barn, but also the horses that were inside.

"I'll call in some men to check out the barn. Do you mind if I bring Jimmy in here to ask him some questions?" Wayne asked.

"That's fine," Eva replied.

Jake was definitely interested in finding out why Jimmy had been hanging around the barn at this time of the night. Although he was grateful the attack had been stopped before Eva had gotten hurt even more, he also found it damned odd that Jimmy had been there at all.

As Wayne stepped outside to get Jimmy, Jake put his arm around Eva and pulled her closer against his side. He could feel small tremors shaking her body, and he hated that she was obviously still so afraid.

"Could you do me a favor?" she asked.

"Of course," he replied.

"Would you go check in on Andy? He saw me when I was crying, and he noticed I was bleeding. I know he's probably in there scared to death right now."

"I'll go talk to him." Jake got up and went down the hallway to Andy's room. He knocked softly and then opened the door.

A night-light illuminated the room enough that Jake could see that Andy was wide-awake. "Mr. Jake," he said and sat up.

"Hey, buddy, how are you doing?" Jake walked over and sat on the edge of the bed.

"I'm okay, but is my mom okay? She was bleeding and she got out her gun."

"She's just fine."

"I heard Sheriff Black here. What happened to my mom, Mr. Jake?"

Jake hesitated a moment before replying. He decided the boy deserved the truth instead of some made-up story. "Somebody bad was hiding in the barn and tried to hurt your mom," Jake explained. "But I'm going to make sure nothing like that ever happens again. Now, what you need to do is get to sleep. You have school tomorrow."

"Maybe I shouldn't go to school." Worry still laced Andy's voice. "Maybe I should stay home to help protect my mom."

Jake smiled at him. "Andy, your job is to go to school, and you need to let the grown-ups take care of your mother. Now everything is fine for the night, so you need to get to sleep."

"Thanks, Mr. Jake." Andy settled back in the bed, and then Jake pulled the sheet up around the boy and leaned down and kissed him on the forehead.

"Stop worrying, Andy. I promise you that everything is going to be just fine."

"I'm glad you came."

"I'm glad I'm here, too. I'm glad you thought to call me. Now, get to sleep." Jake got up and left the room.

He returned to Eva's side just as Wayne led Jimmy into the house. Jimmy immediately looked at Eva. "Are you all right, Mrs. Eva?"

"I will be," she replied.

"I'm so sorry you got hurt. I wish I'd gotten to you sooner." He looked at her mournfully.

"Why were you here at all?" Eva asked.

"I just thought I'd hang around a little later than usual and keep an eye on things. I know somebody

has been causing you bad problems, and I just figured I'd check things out before heading home and
going to bed. I was hoping to catch somebody causing trouble for you so it would all stop."

"Did you see the perpetrator?" Wayne asked.

"No. All I saw was Mrs. Eva on the floor. I wish
I had seen him. I wish I'd caught him," Jimmy exclaimed.

As Wayne continued to question Jimmy, Jake's
mind whirred with a dozen emotions. His heart
ached with Eva's fear. He was afraid for her, too. He
was also enraged by what had happened and angry
that a nine-year-old boy had the burden of being
afraid for his mother's welfare.

He was also suspicious of Jimmy's story. Had the
man orchestrated the attack on Eva and then rushed
in to be a hero? The young man looked at Eva as if
she hung the sun each morning. There was no question he had a crush on Eva. Had he attacked her and
then "saved" her?

Jake spoke those suspicions aloud once Wayne
sent Jimmy home. By that time Wayne's men had
arrived to check out the barn.

"Those same thoughts about Jimmy crossed my
mind, too," Wayne admitted. "At this point everyone
is a suspect. It's too bad Eva didn't see the perpetrator and Jimmy at the same time."

"I just assumed the attacker heard Jimmy's approach and ran away, and then Jimmy showed up,"
Eva replied.

e words left his mouth, he

e hoped Eva didn't fight him
agree to him moving in with
eep in his truck outside her front
mp out in her front yard so that
r her wouldn't get another chance

ached the house, he was about to go
to get his things when David stepped
way and stopped him. "Hey, man, what's
? You've been like a ghost around here."
anie stepped up behind David. "We were
ing a glass of wine before bed. Why don't
in us, Jake? We've scarcely seen you since
e been home."

No, I'm sorry, but I've got to go," Jake replied.

"Go where?" David asked. "Can't you sit and visit
ith us for just a few minutes?"

"I can't. There's been some trouble at Eva's place.
I'm packing some bags and moving in there," Jake
explained.

"Oh Jake," Stephanie said softly.

"What are you doing? Jake, don't you remember
what happened the last time you had anything to do
with her?" David said. "She broke you, man. She totally destroyed you."

"She needs me right now," Jake replied. "She's all
alone in that place with her son, and bad things have
been happening to her."

"But you didn't see which way he ran, right?"
Wayne asked.

"I didn't," she replied.

"And you didn't see exactly where Jimmy came
from, right?" Wayne said.

Eva frowned. "I'm pretty sure he came in the main
barn entrance. It's all so jumbled in my head right
now."

Jake was grateful that the tremors he'd felt in her
earlier were finally gone, but she still appeared small
and achingly vulnerable. Once again Wayne left to
go out and check with his men in the barn.

As he stepped out of the house, Eva released a
weary sigh. "I can't believe this happened. I feel like
I'm in a nightmare, and no matter how hard I try I
can't wake up."

Jake tightened his arm around her. "I'm just grateful you weren't hurt even more. This could have had
a tragic ending."

"Was Andy okay?" she asked.

"He was worried about you, but I told him to leave
the worrying to the grown-ups and that you were
going to be just fine."

"Thank you, Jake." She released a shudder. "The
man wanted to kill me. I believe he really wanted
to kill me." She crossed her arms in front of her so
she was hugging herself. "I…I didn't really think it
would come to this…that the written threats would
become a physical reality."

"I had certainly hoped it wouldn't come to this,"

Jake said. "But now we know just how serious the situation is."

Eva leaned her head back against his arm and closed her eyes. He gazed at her face and vowed to himself that he would do whatever was necessary to keep her and her son safe.

He didn't know how much time passed before Wayne came back into the house. "The deputies are still out there looking for clues, but I came back inside to tell you that it appears somebody was going to set the barn on fire."

Eva sat up straighter. "So I did smell gasoline."

Wayne nodded. "There was a small stack of hay with several pieces of kindling smothered with fuel. All it was waiting for was a lit match. Maybe it was possible you interrupted him attempting to set a fire and that's why he came after you."

"If he didn't really want to hurt her, then why attack her at all? If she interrupted him, then why didn't he just slink away into the night instead of going after her with a pitchfork?" Jake asked. "The barn was dark. No light was on. Hell, he could have hid in a stall until Eva left. So, I repeat, why go after her?"

None of them had the answer. "Have you had a chance to question Robert Stephenson about owning a Kincaid knife?" Eva asked.

Jake gazed at her in surprise. "Why would you think of that right now?"

She told them about Robert and his son joining her and Andy in the ice cream place. "He keeps kind

of ask...
shr...
a...

Wayn...
evidence...
prints. My me...
tooth combs loo...
dropped something...
will help us along."

"There won't be any fin...
her voice sounding hollow. "An...
evidence, either. Whoever is behi...
ally smart."

"They aren't that smart," Wayne protes...
left a knife for us to use to identify them."

"A knife made by a man who sells lots of knive...
Eva replied. She reached up and once again rubbed her temple. "I'm sorry. I'm tired and scared, and I just want this person to be caught."

Jake got to his feet and looked at Wayne. "Can you stay here with Eva until I get back?"

"Sure, but where are you going?" he asked.

"I'm going home to pack a few bags, and then I'm moving in here." He didn't give Eva a chance to

"Let the sheriff protect her," David replied with obvious frustration. "Jake, I don't want to see you hurt by her again. The last time she hurt you, I lost my brother for ten years."

"David, I need to do this, and if I get hurt in the process, so be it. I'm a big boy. Now, I've got to get moving." He didn't wait for his brother to say anything more, instead he thundered up the stairs to his suite.

It was true that when Jake had gone to Italy, his relationship with his younger brother had suffered tremendously. Although they had spoken on the phone and video chatted whenever possible, it hadn't been the same as spending life together on a day-to-day basis.

A half an hour later, he was again in his truck and headed back to Eva's. He understood his brother not wanting him to be involved with Eva again, but there was no way Jake was walking away from her, especially now. No matter what happened between them in the future, he would be there for her right now.

He wanted to protect her from any and all danger. Aside from that, he was hoping they could reclaim the love he believed they'd once had for each other.

This was either going to end with him planning a future with the woman he loved, or he'd suffer the second greatest heartache he'd ever had in his life.

Chapter Nine

The minute Jake got back to the house and dropped two duffel bags inside the front door, there was a part of Eva that wanted him to immediately pick the bags up and go back to his house. However, there was a bigger part of her that was still shaken and frightened and didn't want to be alone.

She figured she'd let him stay with her for the remainder of the night, and then she'd ask him to leave first thing in the morning. There was no real reason for him to move in here permanently.

"I'll get you a pillow and a blanket so you'll be more comfortable," she said to Jake once Wayne and his men were finally gone. "You can sleep out here on the sofa." She steeled herself for him to say something about wanting to sleep with her.

Instead he merely nodded. "That works for me. But I'd like your bedroom door and Andy's door open for the rest of the night. Just in case there is any more trouble. I need to be able to hear you if either of you cry out."

"Don't even tempt fate to bring more trouble here tonight," she replied wearily. "I'm too tired to deal with anything else. I'll be right back." She disappeared down the hallway to get the things for him.

She returned to the living room with a bed pillow and a throw blanket. "Does Andy know about gun safety?" he asked as he took the items from her. He gestured toward his gun, which was now on the coffee table. "I'd like to keep this here for easy access in the night."

"Andy knows his gun safety, and you don't have to worry about him touching your gun," she replied.

"That's good to know. Do you want to go straight to bed, or would you like to talk for a little while? Maybe try to decompress a little bit?" he asked.

"I think I'm ready to go to bed." She released another weary sigh. "I just want to fall asleep and try to forget what happened tonight." Even though she said the words, she knew she couldn't sleep long enough or hard enough to forget the horrifying events of the night.

"How is your leg?"

"It hurts, but not too bad. I did a stupid thing by going to the barn, and I just still feel a little overwhelmed by everything that happened tonight. I'm sure I'll feel much better in the morning."

"I hope so, and I hope you sleep well," he said.

"Thanks. I'll see you in the morning." She turned and walked down the hallway. When she got to Andy's room, she opened the door and was grateful to see that he was sleeping.

She hated that he'd seen her weeping and so scared. She hated that he'd been so frightened he had called Jake. However, she had to admit she'd sleep easier tonight knowing Jake was in the house.

Once she was in her own bedroom, she stripped off her jeans and threw them into the corner. Tomorrow they would make their way into the trash. Even if they hadn't been ruined by the pitchfork, she would have thrown them away anyway.

She then finished undressing and pulled on a cool, short, sleeveless blue nightgown. She peeked out of her room and, not seeing Jake lurking nearby, she hurried into the bathroom, where she washed her face and brushed her teeth.

For several long moments, she stared at her reflection in the mirror. What had she done to warrant the kind of vitriol, the kind of killing rage that somebody had for her? Who was behind these attacks on her? The mirror had no answers to her questions.

Minutes later she was in her bed. She curled up on her side facing the open doorway as the events of the night played and replayed through her mind.

There was no question that with everything that had been going on, she'd been incredibly brainless in going to the barn all alone after dark. But who could have guessed that a man with a pitchfork would come after her?

As her mind filled with a vision of the dark figure with a pitchfork, she shivered despite the warmth of the room. There was a well of iciness inside her that no amount of blankets could warm. It was a cold deep in her soul created from the knowledge that somebody wanted her dead. And that somebody had nearly succeeded tonight.

It had been difficult to explain to Wayne the utter hatred she'd felt emanating from her attacker. It was hard to make the lawman understand that there had been no question in her mind that the attacker wanted to kill her. He hadn't merely been trying to scare her out of the barn. She'd been running away when he'd attacked and used that pitchfork like a weapon to kill.

She finally fell asleep and into fitful dreams of being chased by a masked figure through the night. They were horrid nightmares of near death. It was with relief that she awakened as the sun was just beginning to peek over the horizon.

As she dressed, the scent of fresh coffee wafted from the kitchen, letting her know that Jake was already up. She was far more clearheaded this morning than she'd been the night before.

While she had appreciated his presence in the house last night, she felt confident in sending him home this morning. She was now forewarned that somebody wanted to do her physical harm. She would make sure she didn't make any more stupid mistakes that might put her at risk. But the last thing she needed was Jake in her personal space.

She entered the kitchen and found him seated at the table. He looked far too appealing with his sleep-tossed hair, his bare feet and clad in a white T-shirt and jeans.

"Good morning," he said. "I hope you don't mind. I made some coffee."

"Mind?" She smiled at him. "I thank you." She walked over to the pot and poured herself a cup and then joined him at the table.

"How did you sleep?" he asked.

"Actually, I had a few nightmares," she admitted after a moment's hesitation. "I was glad to wake up and escape from them."

"I'm sorry," he replied, his dark eyes expressing the sentiment. "How does your leg feel?"

"A little sore, but it's okay. How did you sleep?" she asked.

"With one eye open," he replied with an easy grin. "Actually, I found your sofa pretty comfortable."

"That's good." She figured she'd tell him he didn't need to spend another night here after she made breakfast and got Andy off to school. That way if he argued with her, they wouldn't be having the argument in front of her son.

"What do you have on tap for today?" he asked.

"The usual—chores, and I need to go into town for some groceries," she replied. "I refuse to give this person all my power. My daily life certainly can't stop because of all of this going on."

"Of course it can't," he agreed easily. "We all just have to be smarter going forward."

She released a small laugh. "Oh, trust me. I'm

"But you didn't see which way he ran, right?" Wayne asked.

"I didn't," she replied.

"And you didn't see exactly where Jimmy came from, right?" Wayne said.

Eva frowned. "I'm pretty sure he came in the main barn entrance. It's all so jumbled in my head right now."

Jake was grateful that the tremors he'd felt in her earlier were finally gone, but she still appeared small and achingly vulnerable. Once again Wayne left to go out and check with his men in the barn.

As he stepped out of the house, Eva released a weary sigh. "I can't believe this happened. I feel like I'm in a nightmare, and no matter how hard I try I can't wake up."

Jake tightened his arm around her. "I'm just grateful you weren't hurt even more. This could have had a tragic ending."

"Was Andy okay?" she asked.

"He was worried about you, but I told him to leave the worrying to the grown-ups and that you were going to be just fine."

"Thank you, Jake." She released a shudder. "The man wanted to kill me. I believe he really wanted to kill me." She crossed her arms in front of her so she was hugging herself. "I...I didn't really think it would come to this...that the written threats would become a physical reality."

"I had certainly hoped it wouldn't come to this,"

Jake said. "But now we know just how serious the situation is."

Eva leaned her head back against his arm and closed her eyes. He gazed at her face and vowed to himself that he would do whatever was necessary to keep her and her son safe.

He didn't know how much time passed before Wayne came back into the house. "The deputies are still out there looking for clues, but I came back inside to tell you that it appears somebody was going to set the barn on fire."

Eva sat up straighter. "So I did smell gasoline."

Wayne nodded. "There was a small stack of hay with several pieces of kindling smothered with fuel. All it was waiting for was a lit match. Maybe it was possible you interrupted him attempting to set a fire and that's why he came after you."

"If he didn't really want to hurt her, then why attack her at all? If she interrupted him, then why didn't he just slink away into the night instead of going after her with a pitchfork?" Jake asked. "The barn was dark. No light was on. Hell, he could have hid in a stall until Eva left. So, I repeat, why go after her?"

None of them had the answer. "Have you had a chance to question Robert Stephenson about owning a Kincaid knife?" Eva asked.

Jake gazed at her in surprise. "Why would you think of that right now?"

She told them about Robert and his son joining her and Andy in the ice cream place. "He keeps kind of asking me out, and I keep rejecting him." She shrugged her shoulders. "I don't know who to trust anymore. I mean, it could be a couple of teenagers led by Griff, or the father of my son's best friend, or my own ranch hand or somebody else not even on our radar." She seemed to get smaller and smaller with each word.

"We're going to get to the bottom of this, Eva," Wayne said. "I've already taken your pitchfork into evidence. Hopefully we'll be able to pull up some prints. My men are going through the barn with fine-tooth combs looking for any evidence. Maybe he dropped something or left something behind that will help us along."

"There won't be any fingerprints," Eva replied, her voice sounding hollow. "And you won't find any evidence, either. Whoever is behind all this is really smart."

"They aren't that smart," Wayne protested. "They left a knife for us to use to identify them."

"A knife made by a man who sells lots of knives," Eva replied. She reached up and once again rubbed her temple. "I'm sorry. I'm tired and scared, and I just want this person to be caught."

Jake got to his feet and looked at Wayne. "Can you stay here with Eva until I get back?"

"Sure, but where are you going?" he asked.

"I'm going home to pack a few bags, and then I'm moving in here." He didn't give Eva a chance to protest. As quickly as the words left his mouth, he was out her front door.

He drove quickly. He hoped Eva didn't fight him on this. If she didn't agree to him moving in with her, then he would sleep in his truck outside her front door. He would camp out in her front yard so that whoever was after her wouldn't get another chance to hurt her.

When he reached the house, he was about to go up the stairs to get his things when David stepped into the hallway and stopped him. "Hey, man, what's happening? You've been like a ghost around here."

Stephanie stepped up behind David. "We were just having a glass of wine before bed. Why don't you join us, Jake? We've scarcely seen you since you've been home."

"No, I'm sorry, but I've got to go," Jake replied.

"Go where?" David asked. "Can't you sit and visit with us for just a few minutes?"

"I can't. There's been some trouble at Eva's place. I'm packing some bags and moving in there," Jake explained.

"Oh Jake," Stephanie said softly.

"What are you doing? Jake, don't you remember what happened the last time you had anything to do with her?" David said. "She broke you, man. She totally destroyed you."

"She needs me right now," Jake replied. "She's all alone in that place with her son, and bad things have been happening to her."

"Let the sheriff protect her," David replied with obvious frustration. "Jake, I don't want to see you hurt by her again. The last time she hurt you, I lost my brother for ten years."

"David, I need to do this, and if I get hurt in the process, so be it. I'm a big boy. Now, I've got to get moving." He didn't wait for his brother to say anything more, instead he thundered up the stairs to his suite.

It was true that when Jake had gone to Italy, his relationship with his younger brother had suffered tremendously. Although they had spoken on the phone and video chatted whenever possible, it hadn't been the same as spending life together on a day-to-day basis.

A half an hour later, he was again in his truck and headed back to Eva's. He understood his brother not wanting him to be involved with Eva again, but there was no way Jake was walking away from her, especially now. No matter what happened between them in the future, he would be there for her right now.

He wanted to protect her from any and all danger. Aside from that, he was hoping they could reclaim the love he believed they'd once had for each other.

This was either going to end with him planning a future with the woman he loved, or he'd suffer the second greatest heartache he'd ever had in his life.

Chapter Nine

The minute Jake got back to the house and dropped two duffel bags inside the front door, there was a part of Eva that wanted him to immediately pick the bags up and go back to his house. However, there was a bigger part of her that was still shaken and frightened and didn't want to be alone.

She figured she'd let him stay with her for the remainder of the night, and then she'd ask him to leave first thing in the morning. There was no real reason for him to move in here permanently.

"I'll get you a pillow and a blanket so you'll be more comfortable," she said to Jake once Wayne and his men were finally gone. "You can sleep out here on the sofa." She steeled herself for him to say something about wanting to sleep with her.

Instead he merely nodded. "That works for me. But I'd like your bedroom door and Andy's door open for the rest of the night. Just in case there is any more trouble. I need to be able to hear you if either of you cry out."

"Don't even tempt fate to bring more trouble here tonight," she replied wearily. "I'm too tired to deal with anything else. I'll be right back." She disappeared down the hallway to get the things for him.

She returned to the living room with a bed pillow and a throw blanket. "Does Andy know about gun safety?" he asked as he took the items from her. He gestured toward his gun, which was now on the coffee table. "I'd like to keep this here for easy access in the night."

"Andy knows his gun safety, and you don't have to worry about him touching your gun," she replied.

"That's good to know. Do you want to go straight to bed, or would you like to talk for a little while? Maybe try to decompress a little bit?" he asked.

"I think I'm ready to go to bed." She released another weary sigh. "I just want to fall asleep and try to forget what happened tonight." Even though she said the words, she knew she couldn't sleep long enough or hard enough to forget the horrifying events of the night.

"How is your leg?"

"It hurts, but not too bad. I did a stupid thing by going to the barn, and I just still feel a little overwhelmed by everything that happened tonight. I'm sure I'll feel much better in the morning."

"I hope so, and I hope you sleep well," he said.

"Thanks. I'll see you in the morning." She turned and walked down the hallway. When she got to Andy's room, she opened the door and was grateful to see that he was sleeping.

She hated that he'd seen her weeping and so scared. She hated that he'd been so frightened he had called Jake. However, she had to admit she'd sleep easier tonight knowing Jake was in the house.

Once she was in her own bedroom, she stripped off her jeans and threw them into the corner. Tomorrow they would make their way into the trash. Even if they hadn't been ruined by the pitchfork, she would have thrown them away anyway.

She then finished undressing and pulled on a cool, short, sleeveless blue nightgown. She peeked out of her room and, not seeing Jake lurking nearby, she hurried into the bathroom, where she washed her face and brushed her teeth.

For several long moments, she stared at her reflection in the mirror. What had she done to warrant the kind of vitriol, the kind of killing rage that somebody had for her? Who was behind these attacks on her? The mirror had no answers to her questions.

Minutes later she was in her bed. She curled up on her side facing the open doorway as the events of the night played and replayed through her mind.

There was no question that with everything that had been going on, she'd been incredibly brainless in going to the barn all alone after dark. But who could have guessed that a man with a pitchfork would come after her?

As her mind filled with a vision of the dark figure with a pitchfork, she shivered despite the warmth of the room. There was a well of iciness inside her that no amount of blankets could warm. It was a cold deep in her soul created from the knowledge that somebody wanted her dead. And that somebody had nearly succeeded tonight.

It had been difficult to explain to Wayne the utter hatred she'd felt emanating from her attacker. It was hard to make the lawman understand that there had been no question in her mind that the attacker wanted to kill her. He hadn't merely been trying to scare her out of the barn. She'd been running away when he'd attacked and used that pitchfork like a weapon to kill.

She finally fell asleep and into fitful dreams of being chased by a masked figure through the night. They were horrid nightmares of near death. It was with relief that she awakened as the sun was just beginning to peek over the horizon.

As she dressed, the scent of fresh coffee wafted from the kitchen, letting her know that Jake was already up. She was far more clearheaded this morning than she'd been the night before.

While she had appreciated his presence in the house last night, she felt confident in sending him home this morning. She was now forewarned that somebody wanted to do her physical harm. She would make sure she didn't make any more stupid mistakes that might put her at risk. But the last thing she needed was Jake in her personal space.

She entered the kitchen and found him seated at the table. He looked far too appealing with his sleep-tossed hair, his bare feet and clad in a white T-shirt and jeans.

"Good morning," he said. "I hope you don't mind. I made some coffee."

"Mind?" She smiled at him. "I thank you." She walked over to the pot and poured herself a cup and then joined him at the table.

"How did you sleep?" he asked.

"Actually, I had a few nightmares," she admitted after a moment's hesitation. "I was glad to wake up and escape from them."

"I'm sorry," he replied, his dark eyes expressing the sentiment. "How does your leg feel?"

"A little sore, but it's okay. How did you sleep?" she asked.

"With one eye open," he replied with an easy grin. "Actually, I found your sofa pretty comfortable."

"That's good." She figured she'd tell him he didn't need to spend another night here after she made breakfast and got Andy off to school. That way if he argued with her, they wouldn't be having the argument in front of her son.

"What do you have on tap for today?" he asked.

"The usual—chores, and I need to go into town for some groceries," she replied. "I refuse to give this person all my power. My daily life certainly can't stop because of all of this going on."

"Of course it can't," he agreed easily. "We all just have to be smarter going forward."

She released a small laugh. "Oh, trust me. I'm

well aware of that." She took a couple more sips of her coffee and then got up. "Bacon and scrambled eggs for breakfast?"

"Sounds good to me," he replied.

"I'm going to start the bacon, and then I'll get Andy up for school." She pulled a pound of bacon out of the fridge and began to place the slices into a skillet.

"I'd better go clean up before Andy is up," Jake said. "Do you mind if I take a quick shower?"

"Go ahead. Towels are under the sink."

She breathed a little easier as he left the kitchen. He'd looked far too attractive seated at her kitchen table with his morning stubble on his jaw and the early-morning light shining on his dark, sleep-mussed hair.

By the time the bacon was crisp and out of the skillet, Jake came back into the kitchen, smelling of minty soap and his shaving cream. He'd exchanged his T-shirt for a navy blue short-sleeved shirt.

"I'm going to go wake Andy," she said.

"Is there anything I can do to help with breakfast?" he asked.

"Just get yourself another cup of coffee and relax. I've got this." She needed to stay busy, to keep her mind relatively empty, otherwise she'd fall back into the abject fear that she'd felt all night long.

She walked down the hallway and into Andy's room. He was sleeping so peacefully she hated waking him. But he needed to get up and get ready for school.

"Hey, buddy," she said and sank down on the edge

of his mattress. "It's time to get up." She reached out and swept a strand of his dark hair away from his forehead.

His eyes fluttered open, and he offered her a sleepy smile. "Hi, Mom."

"Good morning," she replied. "Breakfast is in fifteen minutes. You need to get up and dressed for school."

He stretched and nodded. She got up and left him. He'd always been easy to get up in the mornings, and she was grateful that this morning was like all the others. However, she knew he had been awake late last night and suspected that he might be in bed a little earlier tonight.

"That didn't take long," Jake said when she returned to the kitchen.

"He's always been an easy kid to get up in the mornings." She got the bread ready to pop down in the toaster and then set to scrambling eggs in a bowl.

"There was a time it took nothing short of a bomb to get me up in the mornings," Jake said. "When I was about Andy's age, it took the housekeepers dozens of efforts to get me out of bed."

She turned and smiled at him. "You never told me that about yourself before."

He laughed. "Thankfully it was something I grew out of. I realized a real cowboy had to be up before dawn, and you know more than anything I wanted to be a real cowboy."

"And now you finally get to be the cowboy you always wanted to be," she replied.

"I do," he agreed. "Although I really won't be completely happy until I'm working on my own ranch instead of the family ranch."

"Would you want to stay around the Dusty Gulch area or head to fresher pastures?" she asked.

"Oh, I'd definitely stay in Dusty Gulch," he replied. "Now that I'm finally back here, I can't imagine living anyplace else."

She poured the eggs into the waiting skillet, and for just a few minutes a comfortable silence reigned between them. His answer to her question about living elsewhere hadn't surprised her. Even as a teenager, Jake had shared with her his love for Dusty Gulch. She'd just popped the bread down to toast when Andy came into the kitchen.

"Mr. Jake! You're still here," Andy said with delight.

"I'm going to be here for a while," Jake replied. "I want to stay here until the bad man who tried to hurt your mother last night is in jail."

"I'm so glad." Andy slid into the chair next to Jake. "If you weren't here, then I'd be really, really worried." Andy looked at Eva as she set his plate before him. "We want Mr. Jake here, don't we? We need him here, right, Mom?"

Eva stared into Andy's worried eyes and felt a sinking sensation in the pit of her stomach. How could she possibly send Jake away now, knowing his presence here made her son feel less afraid?

She would never forget the scared look on Andy's face the night before, and she never, ever wanted to see it again on his beautiful face. And if that meant Jake had to stay here, then she would swallow her discomfort for the sake of her son.

As they ate breakfast, Jake teased Andy and recounted silly times in Jake's own childhood that made Andy laugh over and over again. Eva's heart warmed, and it continued to stay warm as the three of them headed down the lane so Andy could meet his school bus.

This had been Eva's dream at one time…her and Jake together and taking care of their children. She'd once been so certain that it was what her future held. Unfortunately, it had only taken one threat from Justin Albright to change the path of her future.

She shoved these thoughts aside. They had no place in her head anymore. She would put up with Jake being in her personal space for the sake of her son, but that didn't mean she was inviting Jake anywhere near her heart.

THE MINUTE THEY returned to the house, Harley knocked on the back door, and Eva let him in. He looked in surprise at Jake, who had just sunk back down in a chair at the table.

"Good morning, Mr. Albright," he said to Jake.

"Back at you," Jake replied. "And it's Jake."

"Sit, Harley," Eva said. "I'll pour you a cup of coffee."

Harley sat next to Jake and looked at Eva. "Jimmy filled me in on what happened last night. I wanted to come in and see for myself that you were really okay."

Eva set the coffee cup before him and then joined them at the table. "As you can see, I'm fine."

"Thank God for that," Harley replied. "According to Jimmy, you were bloody from head to toe and screaming when he found you."

"That's a bit of an exaggeration, although I was definitely screaming and crying. Whoever was in the barn managed to stab me in the back of my leg with a pitchfork before Jimmy showed up," Eva explained.

Just talking about it darkened her eyes with what Jake knew was fear, and there was nothing he would like more than to have fifteen minutes alone with the attacker. He would beat the man to a bloody pulp for what he'd done to her. He would beat him and then see to it that the person spent the rest of his life in jail. What the perpetrator had done last night was attempted murder.

"Jimmy also told me the person intended on setting a fire in the barn." Harley shook his head. "Thank God that didn't happen. As dry and windy as it's been, the entire barn would have gone up in flames in minutes. I'd sure like to know who the hell is behind all this. I wouldn't mind taking him out behind the barn and beating the hell out of him."

"That makes two of us," Jake replied fervently.

As Harley and Eva began to talk about ranch business, Jake sat back in his chair and studied the man Eva obviously depended on not only as a ranch foreman but also as a friend.

Did Harley have some kind of a secret grudge against Eva?

Harley had access to all the cattle and the barn. After seven years of working for her, he probably knew her routine. He might have been able to guess that she would go into the barn last night.

Had he at some time or another bought one of Kincaid's knives and paid cash for it? And if he had, did he still have that knife, or had he used it to stab a cow's heart into Eva's porch?

Jake frowned and stared down into his coffee cup. He didn't trust anyone right now, and that included the two ranch hands who worked for Eva.

Eva and Harley talked for another fifteen minutes or so, and then Harley left to head out to the pastures.

"I don't know what chores you have to do this morning, but the one thing I don't want you to do is get on the back of a horse and ride around in the pastures," Jake said as soon as Harley had left.

She frowned. "What harm could come from that?"

"Eva, I can't protect you if you're out in an open pasture. If somebody really wants you dead, then all it would take is a bullet," he replied. "And even though I would love for you to believe I'm a superhero, I can't stop a speeding bullet that might be aimed at your head or your heart."

She stared at him for a long moment and then stood and slammed her palms down on the table. "I hate this. I hate being afraid. I hate that my son is afraid, and I'm so angry that my entire life has been turned upside down because of some creep lurking in the shadows." Her eyes blazed with anger.

"I know, Eva, and I'm so sorry for what you're going through." He moved his hands to cover hers. "If I could fix this for you, I would." Her hands were so small and tensed beneath his. "I want this to be over as soon as possible, but right now all I can do is my very best to try and keep you safe."

He felt the tension in her hands slowly soften just before she pulled them away. "I know, and I appreciate it. Am I at least allowed a trip to the grocery store?"

He smiled at her. "I think we can manage that. I'll help you clear up the dishes, and then we can be on our way."

For the next few minutes, they cleaned up the kitchen in silence. He sensed that she wasn't in the mood for idle conversation right now. She worked with a single-minded focus to load the dishwasher and then looked up at him. "I'll go get ready to leave."

Jake went into the living room and pulled on his holster. With his gun hanging from his hip, he felt ready for almost anything...almost.

However, he didn't expect any trouble from just a simple trip into town. Once they arrived there, they would be surrounded by other people, and an attack on Eva where there were witnesses around would be stupid on the perp's part. Unfortunately it was obvious the man wasn't stupid.

His breath caught deep in his throat as she came back into the living room. She'd lengthened her already sinfully long, dark lashes with mascara, and a pink gloss covered her lips. The makeup, coupled with her bright blue blouse and tight jeans, shot his adrenaline just a little bit higher.

"I'm all ready to go," she said.

"You look very nice."

Her cheeks colored a dusty pink beneath his gaze. "Thanks."

They left the house and got into his truck, and he headed toward town. "It's a beautiful day," he said once they'd been driving for a few miles.

"Do you really want to talk about the weather?" she asked wryly.

He flashed her a quick smile. "Not really, but I was afraid of an awkward silence building up between us."

A small laugh escaped her. "And as I remember, you never did like any kind of silence to grow between us."

"I always figured if you got quiet it meant you were mad at me for something," he admitted. "And I could never stand the idea of you being angry with me for anything."

"I fully intended to probably make you angry this morning," she said.

"How so?" He looked at her curiously and then gazed back at the road.

"I had every intention of telling you to take your bags and go back home, that I was fine alone, but then Andy said he felt so much better with you in the house, and now I realize I'm stuck with you."

"Eva, why would you send me home when I'm just another layer of protection for you?" He didn't wait for her to answer. "If you had kicked me out of your house this morning, then I would have camped out in my truck outside your front door in an effort to keep you safe. I don't intend to go away until whoever is after you is in jail."

"Then we need to have rules while you're in the house," she said.

"Rules? What kind of rules?"

"First of all, you need to make sure you're out of the bathroom when it's time for Andy to get ready for school."

"That's an easy rule to follow," he replied agreeably. "What else?"

"You don't try to discipline Andy. If you have a problem with him, you bring it to me, and I'll discipline him."

"Eva, I would never overstep boundaries where Andy is concerned," he said.

"Okay, and last, you sleep on the sofa and you don't try to seduce me to get into my bed."

He laughed. "I can't help it that I'm naturally seductive." He glanced at her in time to see her glare at him.

"I'm being serious here, Jake."

"Okay, I agree to sleep on the sofa and not try to get into your bed. To be honest, I'd sleep on the floor in the hallway if I thought that would keep you safe."

"Thank you, Jake. I really appreciate you doing this, especially since Andy feels so much better with you in the house," she replied.

By that time, they had arrived at the grocery store. They were just about to go inside when they nearly bumped into a man coming out.

"Eva," he greeted her with obvious warmth and then looked at Jake. "Hello, I'm Robert Stephenson." He shifted the grocery bag in his arm and held out his hand to Jake.

"Jake Albright," he replied and shook the man's hand. So, this was Andy's friend's father...the man who had an interest in Eva and was also an owner of a Kincaid knife.

"I was just picking up some snacks for the boys' overnight next Friday," Robert said.

"You should let me contribute to the cause," Eva replied. "It's bad enough it seems lately they are always at your house instead of mine."

"Nonsense," Robert replied, his gaze lingering on her. Jake wanted to tell the man to stop looking at her like she was a tasty treat he'd like to enjoy.

"I never have any trouble with Andy," the man continued. "In fact, I consider him a good influence on my son."

Eva laughed. "That's nice to hear. And I feel the same way about Bobby."

Robert's smile turned into a frown of concern. "Sheriff Black came to my office and spoke to me yesterday. Why didn't you tell me about all the problems you've been having at your ranch?"

"Did Wayne talk to you about a knife?" Jake asked, consciously interjecting himself into the conversation.

"He did, and I showed him my knives. I have a whole collection of Kincaid knives. The handles are so intricately carved, I find them real works of art."

"How many of them do you own?" Jake wanted to know anything that might further the investigation.

"I believe right now I have a dozen."

"How did you pay for the knives you own?" Jake asked.

Robert shot him a cool look. "I explained all that to Wayne. And now I need to get these groceries home. Eva, it's always a pleasure, and it was nice meeting you, Jake."

"I want to talk to Wayne about him," Jake said once Robert was gone and he and Eva were inside the store. "What I'm concerned about is, whoever left that knife in your porch, there's nothing stopping them from buying a replacement to show Wayne."

"Jeez, thanks. You just gave me something else to worry about," Eva said dryly.

"I'm just trying to look at this from all angles," he replied. "And now, let's go buy a cake or some ice cream. I'm in the mood for something sweet."

Their moods lightened as they shopped. It was funny to him that even food brought back memories of the time when they'd been together and he'd eaten most of his evening meals with her and her father.

"Remember that time when you tried to make that soufflé?" he asked as they went up the baking aisle.

She nodded, and her eyes filled with merriment. "I'd been watching a cooking show on television and decided I wanted to start cooking more sophisticated foods."

"And when the soufflé fell flat, you cried like a baby," he replied. She'd cried in his arms, devastated by the cooking failure. "But you've always been an amazing cook."

"That's because my father was a good cook and taught me everything I know," she replied. She released a deep sigh. "I still miss him."

"I don't think grief ever really goes away. If you're lucky and well adjusted, you eventually find a small space in your heart to tuck it away into so you can keep moving forward in your life."

She smiled up at him. "Sometimes, Jake Albright, you can be a very wise man."

He laughed. "I try."

They finished buying the groceries, packed them in the truck bed and then headed for home. Jake had just left the outskirts of town when he glanced in his rearview mirror and saw a pickup truck coming up fast behind him.

Adrenaline fired through him, and he tightened his hands on the steering wheel. "Hold on to your seat. There's a pickup coming up fast on us."

Eva shot a glance out the back window and then looked at Jake. "Do you think whoever is driving it is after me?"

"I don't know," he replied tersely, his gaze divided between the rearview mirror and the road ahead. The suspicious truck kept coming way too fast, and it drew up right on Jake's bumper.

Was it going to try to ram Jake's bumper? Would the driver try to wreck Jake in an effort to get to Eva? Would somebody fire a gun at them? Certainly it was possible somebody could shoot him in order to get to Eva. He could become collateral damage. His stomach clenched tightly as he tried to anticipate what might happen.

Then the offending truck zoomed around them and kept on going.

Both of them expelled sighs of relief as the back of the truck disappeared ahead of them. "I can't believe I got so scared about a truck that was only guilty of speeding," she said.

"Me, too," he admitted. He continued to grip the steering wheel tight. The problem was there was no way for them to guess from what direction danger might come. All he knew for sure was it was coming, and he could only hope that when it came he could stop it before Eva paid a terrible price.

Chapter Ten

Eva, Jake and Andy fell into a routine that Eva found slightly threatening, because it felt so right having Jake in the house.

They ate breakfast together and walked Andy to the bus stop, and then Jake helped her with any chores she had to accomplish. Jake spoke on the phone to his brother and to the foreman of Albright ranching most afternoons while Eva did chores around the inside of the house.

They would then walk back to the bus stop to get Andy, and after that they ate dinner together. Once they finished dinner, Jake helped Andy with his homework while Eva cleaned up the kitchen. There was a lot of laughter in the house—laughter that warmed Eva's heart and made the house feel like a real home.

There had been no more dead cows, and nothing nefarious had occurred since Jake had moved in, and for that Eva was grateful. But she remained on guard, and she knew Jake did, too.

A couple of days of peace certainly didn't mean the danger had passed. Rather, it felt like a wicked countdown to something huge and awful. It was as if there was a clock ticking down to a big explosion.

They were now in the truck and headed into town to drop Andy off for his Friday overnight with Bobby. "I don't know what I'm going to do without you tonight, Andy," Jake said. "What happens if your mom gets mean with me and you aren't there to protect me?"

Andy giggled. "Mom doesn't get mean, and even if she did, I don't know if I could protect you. She'd probably just send me to my room."

Eva and Jake laughed. This was what a real family felt like, she thought as she cast her gaze out the window. Jake filled in a space that had been missing.

It was going to be difficult when the time came for him to go home. Andy would be upset, and Eva had to admit that she would miss him, too. But this had been an arrangement built on desperate need and fear, not want, and she certainly hadn't invited Jake into her life forever.

When they reached town, Eva gave him directions to the Stephenson home. "I'll walk him to the door," Jake said when he'd parked in the driveway of the attractive, two-story home.

"Bye, Mom. I'll see you tomorrow," Andy said as he and Jake got out of the truck.

"Make sure you behave yourself, and I love you," Eva replied.

"Love you, too," Andy said.

Eva watched as the two walked up the sidewalk to the front door. She was shocked to realize father and son had the same gait. Again she thanked her lucky stars that Andy looked more like her than his father.

Robert answered the door, and he and Jake shared a short conversation, then Andy disappeared into the house and Jake returned to the truck.

"He asked how you were doing and if you were okay," Jake said as he slammed the truck door.

"That was nice of him," Eva replied.

"I don't like him. He's way too fixated on you."

Eva laughed. "Jake, he's just a nice man who wanted to go out with me."

"I still don't trust him."

"I don't trust anyone right now except you and Wayne," she replied.

"And that's the way it should be," he said.

As they drove home, their conversation turned to the ranch and her hope to start the barn renovations soon. "I'm planning on hiring Barney Jennings to come out and give me an estimate."

"Who is Barney Jennings?" Jake asked.

"He owns a construction company and has a good reputation for being fair while doing excellent work."

Jake pulled up and parked in front of her house. "How about you wait on that until everything else is resolved? The last thing I want right now is a bunch of men I don't know running around on your property."

"You're right," she replied. "The barn can wait."

Together they got out of the truck and headed inside. "How about some ice cream?" he asked. "I'll fix us each a bowl." He paused in the living room and pulled off his boots. "Ah, that's much better," he said.

"You always looked forward to taking off your boots," she said with a smile.

"Some things never change, and barefoot is always better," he replied with a smile of his own.

Together they went into the kitchen, where she sank down at the table and watched as he prepared two bowls of vanilla ice cream and then covered them with chocolate syrup. He put the bowls on the table and then sat across from her.

"There's nothing better than ice cream on a hot summer night. Hmm, this tastes delicious," she said and then slowly licked the chocolate off the spoon.

She immediately realized her mistake as Jake's gaze on her instantly heated. Suddenly there was a tension between them...a tension that had begun the moment he'd first shown up at her house, a tension that not only had to do with his obvious desire for her, but her own for him.

Her marriage to Andrew had been a sexless one. It had been ten years since she had experienced the sweet slide of a man's kisses against her skin. It had been since her last time with Jake that she had reached the heights of sexual pleasure, since she had felt the unity of complete and total intimacy.

And she suddenly realized she hungered for that

now, and she didn't want it with any other man. She wanted it again with Jake.

What harm could come from making love with Jake one more time? She was determined he would never be in her life long-term, and she'd made that very clear to him. Surely if they were both on the same page, it wouldn't be such a bad thing.

She slowly licked her spoon again, her gaze holding his. "Do you have any idea what you're doing to me right now?" His voice held a deep, husky growl.

"Yes, I think I do," she replied.

He placed his spoon down. "And are you doing it on purpose?"

"Oh, definitely." Her heart beat an unsteady, quickened rhythm as he stood. He reached out and took the spoon from her fingers. He then walked around the table, grabbed her hand in his and pulled her up and out of her chair.

His arms encircled her and pulled her tight against him. The feel of his hard, muscled body against hers thrilled her. His lips crashed down on hers in a kiss that instantly stole her breath away and weakened her knees.

This was what had been missing in her life, this... this passion for another person, this passion that momentarily swept all other thoughts, all other feelings from her mind.

"Eva," he whispered against her ear when the kiss ended. "You know I want you."

"And I want you," she confessed. "But it's just this

one night…just this one time. Jake, I need to know that you understand that."

"I understand," he replied, and then his lips found hers once again.

Somewhere in the back of her mind, she knew this was probably a mistake. She was breaking her own rule that he would never be in her bed again. But a bigger part of her didn't want to deny herself the pleasure of being with Jake just one more time.

This time when the kiss ended, she took him by the hand and led him down the hallway and into her bedroom. The room was warm, but a nice breeze blew in from an open window that made the temperature tolerable.

He pulled her into his arms once again, and as he kissed her, his hands caressed down her back. He cupped her buttocks and pulled her hips firmly against his. He was already aroused, and that only thrilled her more.

She finally stepped back from him and pulled her T-shirt over her head. Neither of them spoke as they continued to undress. She finished first and then slid beneath the pink-flowered sheet on her bed.

She watched as he pulled his T-shirt over his head, exposing his broad, muscled chest. He then quickly got out of his jeans and boxers. Dressed, Jake Albright was a handsome man, but undressed he was sinfully beautiful.

He joined her in the bed and pulled her to him. Being in his arms again was like heaven. She'd spent so many nights over the years thinking and remembering and fantasizing about being with him once again. She'd spent the last ten years being lonely and wanting the loving caresses of a man...this particular man.

He knew each and every place to touch and kiss to bring her the most pleasure. His lips found the area just behind her earlobe that caused small shivers to shoot through her body. "I've missed you so much, Eva," he whispered.

"I've missed you, too," she replied. Oh, she had missed this. She had missed the passion he stirred inside her, the utter desire he evoked in her, a desire that made her remember she was young and alive.

His mouth then slid down the length of her neck and moved from there to one of her breasts, where he sucked and licked her nipple. She softly cried his name as her fingers tangled in his hair.

She was lost in him...in the feel of his warm skin against hers, in the scent of him that dizzied her senses. He licked first one nipple and then the other and a welcome heat formed and swirled around in the pit of her stomach.

His hand slowly slid down her stomach and circled down across her upper thighs, where he languidly stroked.

She raised her hips, already fully aroused and gasping with the need for him. He was also aroused, and she reached down and encircled her fingers around his hard length.

He drew in a deep breath and gently pushed her hand away. "Eva, don't... I won't last if you touch me right now," he said, his voice a husky half groan.

His fingers then found the center of her, and as he stroked her, she arched up to meet his touch. Heat fired through her as exquisite sensations built and built.

Her climax crashed over her, and before she could begin to recover, he moved between her thighs and entered her. Once he was inside her, he froze for a long moment, and their gazes locked.

Jake not only made love with her with his body, but also with his eyes. His eyes burned into hers with such a wealth of desire it was as if he were making love to her on a completely different, breathtaking level. She felt as if he was seeing into her very soul and reading all her secrets and dreams.

Still looking deep into her eyes, he began to slowly stroke in and out of her. She felt connected to him in a way that transcended just their physical act. She had missed this soul connection as much as she'd missed lovemaking.

They moved together like old, familiar lovers and yet with the excitement of two people who couldn't get enough of each other. When they were finished, they collapsed back and waited for their breathing to return to normal.

She released a deep sigh into the crook of his neck, and one of his hands languidly stroked the side of her hip. "I think we just wasted two perfectly good bowls of ice cream," she finally said.

He laughed, and it was a deep, pleasant rumble in her ear. "This was way better than a bowl of ice cream." He leaned down and kissed her forehead.

She knew she should get up and somehow immediately distance herself from him, but she was reluctant to leave the peace and utter contentment she always found in his arms. "Tell me about your life in Italy," she said.

"What do you want to know?" He continued to stroke her hip in a lazy way that furthered her relaxation against him.

"Where did you live? What was your average day like?"

He told her about the luxury villa that he had called home and how every morning he would get up at dawn to drive to the Albright land of grapes and wine making.

"I knew nothing about growing grapes or making good wines when I arrived there. I spent the next month being walked through the operation by the manager, Enrique Bracolla, and then at night I read every book I could find about the process."

"It must have been pretty overwhelming for a nineteen-year-old cowboy from Dusty Gulch," she said.

"Oh, trust me, it was. For the first two years, I completely immersed myself in learning everything I could. I not only wanted to prove myself to Enrique, who was a great mentor and became a good friend, but also to my father. I wanted him to be proud of the man I was becoming."

"I'm sure he was very proud of you, Jake," she said softly.

"I wish I had come back home earlier so that I could have told him goodbye and maybe hear him say that he loved me." He released a short laugh. "But we both know my father wasn't exactly a warm and fuzzy guy."

The last thing she wanted to talk about was Justin Albright. Thoughts of him still brought a bad taste to her mouth, and she certainly couldn't share with Jake the depths of his father's betrayal. It would absolutely break Jake's heart to learn that his father had been such a manipulating monster.

Thankfully the conversation turned to the food in Italy. "The bread was absolutely out of this world," he said. "My cook joked that I was going to turn into a loaf of bread because I ate so much of it. But I also loved the lasagna and all the pastas there, too."

Eva laughed. "If I ate like that, I'd weigh five hundred pounds within the first couple of weeks." She glanced toward the window, where the dark shadows of night had begun to encroach. She froze, her heart seizing in her chest. "Jake, there's somebody at the window watching us," she whispered.

The man wore a ski mask, and his eyes glittered brightly, but she couldn't tell what color they were.

She'd only gotten a quick glimpse of him, and she didn't want to look at him again and scare him off.

"Act natural," Jake said softly and then more loudly. "How about I bring us a couple of new bowls of ice cream?"

"Sounds good to me," she replied, thankful that her voice sounded normal instead of trembling with the fear that shot through her.

As he got out of bed and pulled on his boxers, she slid back beneath the sheet. She felt sick to her stomach knowing that the peeper had seen her naked, had possibly watched as they had made love.

"I'll be right back." Jake left the room, and then complete fear exploded in her chest. What was the man doing at her window? What did he want? And what would happen if Jake approached him?

At one time she'd been in love with Jake the boy, and she suddenly realized at that moment she was in love with Jake the man. And now the man she loved was about to confront somebody evil. She could only pray he came back to her unharmed.

JAKE HURRIED INTO the living room, where he yanked on his cowboy boots, grabbed his gun off the coffee table and then flew out the front door. Adrenaline shot through him as he slowly crept to the corner of the house. He turned the corner and continued creeping to the next corner.

He held his gun tightly, unsure what to expect. What was the person doing looking in Eva's bedroom window? Was he hoping to catch her alone in the room so he could shoot her? Break through the window and strangle her?

When he turned the next corner, he saw the man still at her window. He must have made a sound, for the man turned his head, saw Jake and then took off running.

Jake pursued, pushing himself to run as fast as possible in an effort to catch the offender. He had to catch him. He needed to know who it was and what he was doing outside Eva's window.

He followed the man into the pasture, and the darkness of night slammed down all around, making it more difficult for Jake to keep the dark figure in his eyesight.

He wanted to shoot the man, but he knew a bullet in the back of a window peeper would only get Jake a long prison sentence. It was one thing to shoot a man in self-defense, but quite another to shoot a retreating man.

Sweat popped out on his forehead, and his muscles tried to cramp, but still he pushed forward. He had to slow down as he now had the obstacles of Eva's cattle to contend with.

"Dammit," he said on a gasp as he finally stopped running. There was no way he was going to catch the man now, and in any case, he'd lost sight of him. He leaned over with his hands on his knees as he panted from his efforts.

A wealth of frustration weighed heavily on his

shoulders. He hated like hell that he hadn't been able to catch the man. He had certainly been the person they had all been looking for...the man who wanted Eva dead. All he had was a general impression of the perp. He'd been tall and with an average build, hardly enough to specifically identify him.

Finally catching his breath, he straightened, and a horrifying thought shot through his head. Had the man at the window wanted to be seen, knowing that Jake would come after him?

While Jake had been running around out in the pasture, had another man gone into the house? Had it been a scheme to get Eva all alone?

God, he'd left the front door not only unlocked but open when he'd raced out of the house. Eva had been naked in her bed, potentially a vulnerable victim to whoever might come into the house.

With all kinds of horrible visions of what could happen, what might have already happened, burning in his brain, he took off running toward the house in the distance.

Was it possible it wasn't just one person behind all the attacks? He immediately thought of Griff and his band of teenage friends. But would teenagers really set out to murder a woman because she'd objected to them partying in her barn?

Visions of news stories concerning the terrible crimes committed by teenagers flashed in his mind. Yes, it was possible teenagers could plot and carry out a murder.

None of that mattered right now. He just had to get to Eva. He ran all out, as if his very life depended on it. And it did, for if Eva was hurt or worse while on his watch, he'd never, ever be able to forgive himself.

His side hitched and his breath became gasps as he raced. His heartbeat thundered not only from his exertions, but also from fear.

As he rounded the corner to the house, he saw that the front door was shut. Was somebody right now inside there with Eva? He got to the door and found it locked. "Eva," he shouted and banged on the door with his fist.

The door opened, and she stood there, her eyes wide with fear, but she was unharmed. "Thank God." He grabbed her to him, needing to feel her in his arms to ensure himself that she was really okay.

"I was about to say the same thing," she said. "I was so scared for you."

He released her and then closed and locked the door. He led her over to the sofa, where they both sank down. She was now clad in a lightweight white robe.

"Needless to say, I didn't catch the guy," he said, frustration pressing tight against his chest.

She placed a hand on his arm. "It's okay. I'm just glad you're back here safe and sound."

"I'd rather have the man in my custody and Wayne on the way to arrest him." He clenched his hands as he remembered how badly he'd wanted to shoot the man.

"Speaking of Wayne, do we really need to call him out about this?"

"It's your call," he replied. "The man is obviously long gone, and I don't have any real details that would help identify him."

"Neither do I. I think we can wait until tomorrow and just let Wayne know this occurred," she replied.

"I definitely think we need to change some things around here," he said.

"Like what?" She looked at him curiously.

"From now on, we need to keep all windows down and locked, and the shades need to be pulled down tight. I don't want anyone to be able to look in and see where we are or what we're doing in this house."

Color crept into her cheeks. "I can't believe that creep saw me naked."

"Yeah, I don't like that, either," he replied with a touch of anger. He hated that anyone except him had seen Eva's beautiful body.

He released a weary sigh. "I need a shower. I worked up a sweat running through the pasture, but first let's get all the windows closed and locked and the shades pulled down."

Together they went around the house and drew curtains and pulled down blinds. "When you get finished with your shower, I'll take one, and then I don't know about you, but I'm ready for bed."

He'd love to ask her if she wanted to shower together, but he sensed she needed a bit of distance.

Besides, they were both still processing more than a little fear.

"Why don't you go shower first," he suggested. "I know how long it takes for your hair to dry."

She nodded and headed for the bathroom. With the sound of the water running, he once again walked around the house, rechecking windows and doors to make sure everything was locked down tight.

He had no idea why the man had window peeped. What had he hoped to gain by watching Eva's bedroom? After dead, mutilated cattle and a bloody heart left hanging from the porch rail, a window peeper seemed rather benign. So, what did it mean?

The shower stopped running, and minutes later Eva left the bathroom clad in a short, sleeveless nightgown that perfectly matched her violet eyes. She carried with her a hairbrush and a dryer.

"I can dry my hair in here," she said. She plugged her dryer into a nearby socket and then sank down on the sofa.

"I'll just be a few minutes. Needless to say, don't open the door to anyone."

"Ha, like that would happen." She turned on the hair dryer, and he went into the bathroom for his shower.

As he stood beneath the warm spray of water, his mind still worked to make sense of what had happened. But there was no way he could reason through it. And that worried him. This all worried him a lot.

The investigation had come to a grinding halt as

no new clues had come to the surface. It was difficult to figure out who was behind a crime when nobody knew why it was happening.

Who was after Eva and why? That was the question that needed to be answered. If they could figure
out the why, then maybe they'd be able to figure out
the who. But right now there were just simply no answers.

He finished with his shower and pulled on a fresh
pair of boxers and then returned to the living room,
where Eva was brushing out her hair. He sat next
to her. "Let me," he said and took the brush from
her hand.

She turned her back toward him, and he stroked
the brush through her long hair, loving the feel of the
silky strands against the back of his hand. "I always
loved to brush your hair," he murmured.

She dropped her head back. "I always loved it
when you brushed my hair."

Initially he'd felt the tension radiating from her,
but the longer he brushed, the more relaxed she became. They didn't speak. No words were necessary.

She finally released a big yawn. "You'd better stop
now, or I'll fall asleep right here." She stood and took
the brush from him.

"Are you going to force me to sleep on this lumpy,
uncomfortable sofa tonight?" he asked.

She narrowed her eyes. "You told me the sofa was
surprisingly comfortable."

"Your bed would be far more comfortable," he replied. "I know it would just be for this one time, Eva. Let me go to sleep tonight with you in my arms."

She held his gaze for a long moment and then nodded. "As long as you understand this is a one-time thing."

Together they went into the bedroom and got into bed. He placed his gun on the nightstand and then turned out the bedside lamp, plunging the room into darkness.

He pulled her into his arms, spooning her against him. She snuggled in, and his love for her beat full in his heart. Tonight filled him with hope that there really was a future for them, that they could be the family he'd always wanted.

All he had to do was keep Eva alive.

Chapter Eleven

It had been almost a week since Eva had made love with Jake, and in the last week, she had tried to distance herself from him. However, it was difficult when she watched him interacting with Andy. He was so patient and loving with him, and she'd seen Andy blossom even more beneath Jake's attention.

He was the father she had always wanted for her son, the kind of man she would want in their lives forever. But it could and would all explode if he ever found out Andy was really his son.

He would hate her for the lies of omission, for the secret she had kept not only for the past nine years but had continued to keep from him when he'd arrived back in town. There was no way they could have a future together. Still, that didn't stop her from needing him now.

"It's nice that the weather hasn't been as hot the last couple of days," he now said.

They had just seen Andy off on the school bus and were now walking back to the house. "I'm just glad it's been another quiet week. No dead cows in the pasture and no cow hearts showing up anywhere. Isn't it crazy that the absence of those things makes it a good week?"

"It isn't crazy, it's tragic," he replied.

They had just reached the house when Wayne's car pulled up into the driveway. They waited for him to park and get out of the car.

"Morning," he said. "I've finally got some information for you." He carried a handful of papers with him.

"Come on in," Eva said. There was nothing about Wayne's demeanor that got her excited about whatever information he might have. All she really wanted to hear from the lawman was that the person terrorizing her was behind bars.

She wanted an end to her fear. Once the perp was in jail, then she'd be able to send Jake home and get the real distance from him she knew she desperately needed. She suspected she was only clinging to him right now because she was still afraid. And that wasn't fair to him or to her.

Eva poured Wayne a cup of coffee and then joined the two men at the table. "What have you got for us?" She gestured to the paperwork in front of Wayne.

"I finally got the names of people who charged the purchase of a Kincaid knife from all three of the convenience stores that sell them." He scooted the papers in front of Eva. "I thought you'd want to take a look at them and see if anyone looks suspicious. I did find one purchase a little telling."

"Which one?" she asked.

"I'd rather you find it for yourself," Wayne replied and then leaned back in the chair and took a sip of his coffee. "I had the stores go back a full year."

Eva picked up the first sheet of paper and began to read down the list of names. "I recognize several people, but nobody I know well," she said when she'd finished with the first page. She handed the list to Jake and then began to read the second page.

Her heart stopped on one particular name. "Wilma Ainsley? Griff's mother bought a Kincaid knife? Was this the one Griff supposedly lost in my barn?" She looked up at Wayne.

"Look at the date on that purchase," Wayne said.

A small gasp escaped her. "Two days after we confronted Griff about his lost knife." She looked from Wayne to Jake.

Jake's jaw tightened. "So, his mother was attempting to muddy the water by being able to show that Griff had his Kincaid knife."

"Either that or Griff used his mother's credit card, which is entirely possible," Wayne replied. "In any case, it makes him look damned suspicious."

"So, what are you thinking?" Jake asked Wayne.

"I'm really beginning to think this has all been the work of Griff and a couple of his friends. It wouldn't be a difficult task for a few big, burly teenagers to kill a cow or hang that cow heart on your porch. The peeping incident sounds more like a teenage stunt than an adult who wants to kill you."

"What about the attack in the barn?" Eva asked. Although her wounds had healed up, she certainly hadn't forgotten the terror she'd felt in the moment.

"I still think it's possible you were attacked because you interrupted the person who was going to set a fire," Wayne replied.

"So, if you think Griff and some of his friends are responsible for all this, then what do you intend to do about it?" Jake asked.

"Now I need to prove it," Wayne replied. "This afternoon I'm going to interview several of Griff's closest friends. I think if I lean on them hard enough, one of them will break and confess to everything."

"Let's hope that happens," Eva replied. It gave her a little relief to think that everything that had happened to her had been at the hands of a bunch of teenagers causing mischief, albeit terrifying mischief.

"I'll let you know how it goes later this evening," Wayne said and stood. "I'll definitely be talking to Griff again about the purchase of another knife."

"Makes him look guilty as hell in my mind," Jake said as they walked Wayne to the door.

"What are you thinking?" Jake asked once Wayne had left and the two were back in the kitchen.

She leaned with her back against the counter that held the remnants of the pancakes she'd made earlier for breakfast. "I'm thinking that if this all really was the work of teenagers, then I'm not quite as afraid as I've been."

She turned around and began to clean up the dishes. If what Wayne now believed was true, then she didn't think the teenagers would actually follow through to murder her. She finished with the dishes and then turned to look at Jake, who was seated at the table.

"Maybe I'm not in as much danger as I thought I was in and it would be okay if you went back to your home now," she said.

"But what if Wayne is wrong?"

His words hung in the air, and Eva frowned as she considered what he'd said. What if Wayne was wrong about Griff and his friends and she sent Jake home? As much as she wanted to distance herself from Jake, ultimately she was afraid to send him home until this horrifying mystery was solved.

"You told me you were sure that the person in the barn wanted to kill you," he continued. "Does it really matter whether it was a teenager or not? Whoever was in the barn that night is still out there somewhere."

"Point taken," she finally replied.

The truth was she wouldn't feel completely safe until somebody was behind bars. If nothing else, she had to think of her son. If anything happened to her, what would become of Andy? It was a question she didn't even want to entertain at the moment.

"If you have any dirty clothes, I'm going to do laundry this morning." She needed to keep herself busy and out of her own head. She needed the mundane of her life right now. She was mentally and emotionally exhausted from being afraid. "In fact, I'm going to spend the day doing some major housework."

"What can I do to help?" he asked.

"Nothing, just stay out of my way and let me do my thing."

"Then I'll just sit here and make some phone calls. I'll check in with David and then talk to Enrique to make sure there are no problems with the winery. I'm also talking to several people who might be interested in buying the winery if we decide to sell."

"That's great—now, dirty clothes?"

"I do have some things, but you shouldn't have to do my laundry all the time."

"Nonsense," she replied.

Minutes later she loaded the washer and got it running, then went back into Andy's room. Once there she stripped the sheets off his twin bed and tossed them into a pile in the doorway for the next load of laundry and then went to work polishing nightstands and the bookcase.

A smile curved her lips as she moved Andy's treasures that he kept on the shelves. There was the special rock shaped like a dragon and a large feather from an eagle. There was also a collection of arrowheads he had found around the ranch and a handful of drawings he'd accomplished in the last week or two.

Andy was a talented little artist, and she grabbed the handful of drawings and sank down on the edge of the bed to look at his latest creations.

Her smile widened at the first drawing, which depicted a boy and a dog—beneath it was written the caption Please, Mom. She could only assume eventually the drawing would make its way to her bedroom, where she would be sure to see it.

Maybe it was time to really think about a puppy for her son. When Jake went back home, it would be the perfect opportunity to get a dog that would hopefully take Andy's thoughts off the absence of Jake in their lives.

There were several more drawings of horses and wildlife, and then she gazed at the last one, and her heart constricted tight. It was a depiction of the backs of two people...a boy and a man. They walked side by side and had fishing poles over their shoulders.

It wasn't how the boy leaned into the man that squeezed her heart, nor was it the way the man had his arm around the boy's shoulders. It was the caption beneath that nearly gutted her. The man I want for a dad and me.

She quickly put the drawings back in order and placed them back on the shelf. As she dusted the rest of the furniture in the room, her heart held a deep sadness for her son.

He was going to be devastated when Eva finally shoved Jake out of their lives forever. There was no way she could fix the decisions she'd made so long ago so now they could all have a happily-ever-after ending. And somehow she didn't think a new puppy was going to help.

JAKE HUNG UP the phone after talking to David for some time. He was glad David was on board with the sale of the winery and had indicated Jake should go ahead with talking to any prospective buyers. They had agreed on a price that was way above what their father had paid for the winery fifteen years ago. Their conversation had then moved on to the ranch business. Jake was staying in touch with the ranch foreman, Bailey Turrel, who had been taking care of things for the past ten years.

Jake told his brother he intended to get more involved with the ranch once the issues at Eva's place were resolved. David once again told Jake how much he worried about Eva playing games with Jake's heart, and Jake assured his brother he had a handle on things where Eva was concerned.

He knew his brother meant well, but Jake didn't want to hear anything negative about being around Eva again, and so he cut that particular subject short.

This time with Eva and Andy had been wonderful. He felt like he'd finally found his home. Of course he would have loved to be sleeping with Eva in her bed every night, but currently he was just trying to prove he was the right man for her and that he belonged here forever.

But first they needed to catch a predator and put him behind bars. If that person was Griff, then he and whoever had helped him in terrorizing Eva needed to be in jail for a very long time. Jake was hoping that once the danger element was removed from her life, she'd realize she was in love with him again and that they deserved to live the future they had once dreamed about together.

As she started vacuuming the living room, he stepped outside the front door. His gaze shot in all directions, always looking for potential trouble.

In the distance Harley and Jimmy were on horseback in the pasture. Jake had come to like and trust Harley, who seemed to look at Eva like a daughter and wanted only the best for her. He was certainly less trustful of Jimmy, especially since the barn incident. Still, his money was on Griff. It was damning that he had gone out to buy another knife after being questioned about the one he'd owned.

What he hoped for was that by the time evening fell that night, the guilty party would be behind bars. He hated the whisper of fear that never quite left Eva's eyes. He hated that she was never able to completely relax.

One thing he did believe, even though she hadn't accepted it herself, was that she loved him. He saw it in the gazes she shot his way when she thought he wasn't looking. He felt it in the way she touched him. They felt like lingering caresses when she took the dirty dishes from him or whenever they inadvertently touched.

Yes, he truly believed she was in love with him, but she couldn't move forward because of the danger that filled her head and heart. He recognized there just wasn't room in her heart for him right now. He'd spent the last ten years loving Eva, and he could be very patient in waiting for her now.

As he watched Harley and Jimmy disappear from sight, he was grateful that once again there had been no dead cows to contend with this morning. In fact, nothing had happened since the man in the ski mask had peeped through the bedroom window. Was it because Griff knew they were on to him?

The weather had been pleasant earlier, but now there was a building heat and an uncomfortable thick humidity. He turned and went back into the house, where Eva had stopped vacuuming and had disappeared into her bedroom. He walked down the hallway and saw her preparing to put clean sheets on her king-size bed.

"Let me help you," he said and moved to the opposite side of the bed from her.

"Thanks. This is the one job I always hate doing by myself." She threw him half of the fitted bottom sheet.

"I can make it so you never, ever have to do this job alone again," he replied, keeping his tone light and teasing.

"Just fit the sheet on, buddy," she replied.

He laughed. "You know I can be as handy as a pocket in a shirt to have around. You'd never need a back scratcher again or a stepladder for those high shelves in the kitchen."

"My back rarely itches, and I like my stepladder,"

she countered as she threw half of the top sheet toward him.

He laughed again. "You get a special price at the café for a family-style meal. Speaking of...why don't we get out of here and have dinner at the café this evening?"

She tucked in the sheet and straightened. "Oh, I don't know..."

"Come on, Eva. We've been cooped up here in the house for a couple of weeks now. A change of scenery for a little while would be good for us all." He'd love to take her out and display her proudly on his arm.

She grabbed the peach-colored bedspread off the nearby chair and threw it onto the bed, then straightened once again and blew a strand of her hair out of her eyes.

"Actually, dinner out sounds good. Andy always likes to eat at the café." A trace of fear darted into her eyes.

"Maybe it will be a celebration dinner if Wayne manages to break down Griff and his friends and they all confess they've been behind everything."

"That would really be wonderful."

"Why don't we plan on heading out of here around five," he said as they finished straightening the bedspread.

"Sounds good. That will give me time to finish with my cleaning and then get ready to go out."

"Ah, yet another reason to keep me around. I can cut your workload in half."

"Jake, I'm warning you." She picked up one of the pillows from the bed, her eyes suddenly filled with a teasing glint.

"If I was here all the time, you'd never get cold in the winter, because I'd be your snuggle mate."

The pillow flew across the bed and smacked him in the face. "I warned you," she said with a laugh.

"Ah, this means war," he said. He walked around the bed and then threw the pillow back at her, hitting her in the chest.

Within seconds they were in an all-out pillow fight. Their laughter filled the room, and laughing with Eva felt so damned good. They laughed even louder when one of the pillows split open and feathers flew everywhere. He finally grabbed her around the waist and pulled her down to the bed.

For a long moment they simply gazed at each other as they tried to catch their breaths. He plucked several feathers from her hair and grinned. "I win," he finally said.

She returned his smile. "You won by breaking my pillow."

He laughed. "I'll help you clean up the mess, but first I want my prize for winning the battle."

One of her dark eyebrows crooked upward. "And what prize do you think you deserve?"

"At the very least, my prize should be a kiss." He half expected her to buck him off her, but instead her eyes darkened and her breath once again quickened.

"Okay, one simple kiss," she said.

He covered her mouth with his. There was nothing simple about kissing Eva. As his tongue sought entry, every part of his body was engaged in the kiss. His heartbeat accelerated, and his arms ached to wrap her up and pull her closer. He was instantly aroused as he deepened the kiss.

She allowed it for only a couple of seconds and then turned her head and shoved at his chest. "Okay, winner, your prize has been paid." He immediately stood and then pulled her up to her feet.

"I need to get this mess all cleaned up," she said.

"I'll help," he replied. "As handy as a pocket in a shirt."

"Start picking up feathers," she replied with a laugh.

Jake's heart squeezed with love. If this didn't end the way he wanted, then he would never be the same again.

At ten till five, Andy and Jake sat in the living room, waiting for Eva to be ready to go out to dinner. "You think maybe I could get a piece of chocolate cake for dessert tonight?" Andy asked.

"You can have whatever you want," Jake replied with a smile to the boy who had crept so deeply into his heart. "If you want two pieces of chocolate cake, then you can have them after you eat your vegetables."

"That's okay. I don't mind eating some vegetables, but I hate brussels sprouts."

Jake laughed. "I hate them, too."

"Mr. Jake, is the bad man that hurt Mom going to get caught and put in jail?"

"I really hope so, buddy. I know Sheriff Black is working real hard to make that happen." Once again Jake was angered by the fear he saw in Andy's eyes. Damn the person doing all this to Eva and making Andy collateral damage.

"We're going to get him, Andy," he assured the boy. "You just need to stay strong for your mother until that happens."

At that moment Eva came into the room. She looked absolutely stunning in a pair of jeans and a violet blouse that showcased her slender waist and full breasts and perfectly matched her eyes. God, he was so proud to be the man by her side.

"You look very pretty," he said.

"Yeah, Mom, you look really good," Andy echoed.

"Thank you," she replied. "I don't know about you two, but I'm starving."

"Me, too," Andy replied.

They left the house, and the heavy humidity pressed tight. It felt like storm weather, and in fact the forecast was for thunderstorms to make an appearance later on in the night.

Minutes later the three of them were in Jake's truck and talking about what they intended to order to eat. For Jake, it was just another wonderful glimpse into what could be if he and Eva were together again.

"I think I'm in the mood for a big, juicy steak," Jake said.

"Me, too," Andy replied. "What are you going to get, Mom?"

"I'm not sure, but I'm leaning toward the chicken-fried steak with mashed potatoes and gravy," she replied.

"You always get that," Andy protested.

Eva laughed. "I just know what I like."

The Dusty Gulch Café was a popular place to eat. The food was good, the prices were reasonable, but more importantly, it was a great place for the gossipers in town to gather.

Jake felt the stares that followed the three of them as they made their way to an empty booth toward the back of the café. This was really the first time he and Eva had made an appearance together. The grocery store didn't count. The café appearance made it more official.

Jake took the side of the booth where he could see who came into the café and who might approach them. He definitely didn't want any surprises. Andy sat next to him and across from his mother.

They placed their orders, and then while they waited Andy kept them entertained with stories about what had happened at school that day. "Jeffrey brought his pet frog today and it jumped out of the box he had it in." Andy's eyes sparkled with merriment. "The girls all screamed and got up on their chairs, and the boys were all running around the room and trying to catch it."

"Who finally caught it?" Eva asked.

"Jeffrey did and Mrs. Roberts told him to never bring the frog again, but then she had us all write a story about Mr. Frog's adventures."

"And what did you write about?" Jake asked.

"My frog was a cowboy who lived in the pond and rode the range during the days on his favorite dog." Andy slid a sly look at his mother. "Frog took good care of his dog without his mother's help and they were best friends."

Eva smiled at her son. "I got the point, Andy," she said with a small laugh. "I might see a dog in your future, but first we have to decide what kind of a dog you want."

At that time their meals arrived, and the conversation turned to different kinds of dogs. They discussed the pros and cons of different breeds and whether Andy wanted a big dog or a smaller one, an indoor dog or an outdoor one.

They were almost finished eating when Robert Stephenson and his son walked through the door. Andy immediately spied his friend and waved to him.

Robert guided his son back to their booth. "Jake... Eva," he greeted them. "Eva, I'm glad to see somebody can get you to take a break and get a meal out," he said. Where before Jake had seen warmth in Robert's eyes when he looked at Eva, tonight Jake swore he detected a hint of coolness there.

Jake was also beginning to wonder if Robert had been stalking Eva. He and his son seemed to show up wherever Eva went.

Eva's cheeks warmed with color. "Jake twisted my arm to come out this evening," she replied.

"Bobby and I are doing takeout. I suggest you all finish up pretty quickly—the weather is looking pretty nasty out there," Robert said. "We're now under a tornado watch until three in the morning."

Storms in Kansas weren't anything to take lightly. A tornado could level a town in a matter of minutes. "Maybe we should take Robert's advice and get done and get home," Eva said as a worried frown slid across her forehead.

The three of them finished up quickly and then stepped out of the café. The air was sultry and still and there was no sign of the moon or the stars in the dark, cloudy sky.

"I don't mind storms, but I really hate bad storms," Eva said softly enough that Andy wouldn't hear her in the back seat.

"We'll keep an eye on it, and if we have to go to your storm cellar then we'll go," he replied.

He knew she had a storm cellar right outside the back door. The last time he'd been in the small space, it had contained shelving holding canned goods and a cot. If necessary, the three of them could escape a storm's wrath by going there and hunkering down for the duration of the weather event.

They arrived back home and turned on the television, where the tornado-watch box was at the bottom of the screen. The details of the watches and warnings scrolled across.

The three of them played a card game until it was time for Andy to shower and call it a night. When he'd been sent off to bed and had been tucked in, Eva and Jake sank down on the sofa.

The television station had now canceled all regular programming, and the local weatherman had taken over the screen. There were tornadoes spinning up all around the area. Storm chasers were active and checking in on a regular basis with reports of damage on the ground.

"I'm not going to sleep until all this weather has settled down for the night. We haven't seen this kind of active weather pattern for a long time," she said. "If you want to go ahead and go to sleep, I'll move to the chair and turn down the volume on the TV and try to be as quiet as possible."

"You can sit right here. I'll stay up with you. Another reason to have me around all the time—I would always be your storm-watch buddy."

She shot him a whisper of a smile and then turned a worried look back to the television. The minutes turned into hours as they talked and watched the weather reports. Occasionally he got up and went to the front door to peer outside.

Thunder clapped and lightning slashed through the dark sky. The wind whipped tree branches into a frenzy. It felt like a night of evil, and Jake wasn't only looking at the weather elements but also keeping watch for trouble of the human sort. Under the cover of a storm, a lot of madness could occur.

There had been no word from Wayne, and so he suspected the teenagers had remained strong through his interviews. That left a lot of uncertainty. Either that or the teenagers truly weren't guilty, which was even more troubling.

It was two thirty in the morning when the weather finally cleared up. Eva released a big yawn and struggled to her feet. "I'm totally exhausted," she said.

"Yeah, I'm pretty tired myself," he admitted. "I can't remember the last time I was up this late."

"Me, neither. Good night, Jake. Thank you for seeing me through the storm." She offered him a sleepy smile.

"Anytime," he replied.

He watched until she disappeared into her room, and then he went to the front door, opened it and stepped out on the porch. The air smelled fresh and clean after the rain they had received. Stars had begun to show back up in the sky, an indication that the dark clouds had finally moved away.

He looked around and, seeing nothing that disturbed him, he turned and went back into the house. *Thank you for seeing me through the storm.* Her words echoed in his mind as he stretched out on the sofa.

He'd seen her through this particular storm, but there was another one coming. A storm of a different kind, and he could only pray that he would see her through that one, too.

Chapter Twelve

Eva awoke slowly, her brain begging for just a little more sleep. She hadn't been up so late since Andy was born. Sleepiness kept her eyelids closed for several more long minutes.

She finally opened her eyes. With the shades pulled at the windows, no morning sun filled the room to help her wake up or know exactly what time it might be.

She rolled over and eyed the clock on her nightstand. Alarm pulled her upright. She'd overslept, and if she didn't get up and get moving right now, Andy was going to be late for school. And he was a boy who absolutely hated being late.

There was no scent of coffee in the air, which let her know Jake had overslept as well. She got out of bed and raced into the living room, which was also semidark because of the shades all being pulled.

He was still sound asleep. "Jake," she said urgently.

He shot up and fumbled on the side table for his gun. "What's up?"

"We've overslept. Andy is going to be late for school if we don't get moving."

He immediately got up from the sofa. "What do you need for me to do?" he asked and raked a hand through his unruly hair.

"If I can get Andy ready in time for him to catch his bus, then you don't need to do anything. But if he misses the bus, could you drive him to school?"

He frowned, and she knew what he was thinking. "Jake, it's seven thirty in the morning—I'm sure I'll be fine here for the twenty minutes or so you would be gone. And now I need to get Andy up and moving," she said, aware of the time ticking by.

She hurried down the hallway and into Andy's bedroom. "Andy...honey, we're late. I overslept. You need to get up and dressed as quickly as you can so you aren't late for school."

"Okay," he said and sat up.

"I'll make you something for breakfast, but you'll have to eat fast." She left his room and hurried into the kitchen, where Jake was starting coffee.

"Andy hates to be late to school," she said as she pulled a skillet out from the cabinet.

"Calm down, Eva. Right now it's possible he might miss his bus, but if we leave here in the next fifteen minutes or so, I can get him to school without him being tardy." He turned to look at her. "You know I don't like the idea of leaving you here alone."

She sprayed the skillet, turned on the burner and then cracked an egg into it. "I'm sure I'll be fine for no longer than you'll be gone. There's no way I can get myself ready to leave this house and still have Andy make it to school on time."

She flipped the egg over.

"I can't believe I overslept so much," Jake said. He got a to-go cup from the cabinet along with a regular coffee cup.

"We both had a really late night," she replied. "And it doesn't help that all the blinds are pulled and it feels like twilight in here."

Andy came into the kitchen just as Eva finished putting together an egg sandwich for him. "Jake is going to take you to school. You can eat this on the way."

She wrapped the sandwich in a paper towel, and Andy took it from her. Jake grabbed the to-go cup of coffee he'd prepared, and then the three of them headed for the front door.

She kissed Andy's forehead. "Sorry for the rush this morning. Just have a great day at school."

"I will, Mom," he replied with a bright smile. "I'll see you later."

She watched from the front door as Jake and Andy got into Jake's truck and then it disappeared down the lane. She closed and locked the door behind them and then released a deep sigh.

She'd been in frantic mode since the moment she had opened her eyes and seen the clock on the nightstand. She shoved a hand through her messy hair and headed back into the kitchen.

She hadn't even managed to get out of her nightgown, but all she wanted now was to relax for a few minutes and drink a cup of coffee. She'd clean up and get dressed after she had her coffee.

She sank down at the table with the cup that Jake had fixed for her before he'd left. She took a sip and leaned back in the chair.

Last night while she and Jake had been weather watching, they had talked about a lot of things. He'd told her about his brother, David, whom Eva remembered from high school, and his wife, Stephanie, whom Eva had seen around town but had never officially met.

He talked about how much he liked his sister-in-law and how he hoped to foster a good relationship with his nephew. Eva knew how important family was to Jake. Now with his father gone, she hoped he'd really be able to build those family bonds with his brother and his wife and children that would feed his soul.

The one thing they hadn't talked about was the past, for which she was grateful. Besides, they had built a new relationship now, one as adults instead of teenagers filled with nothing but youthful hopes and dreams.

She finished drinking the cup of coffee and then decided it was time to get up and get cleaned up for the day. She was about to get out of the chair when a shadow of a person moved across her back door.

Maybe it was Harley ready for their daily check-in.

God, she hoped he hadn't found any more mutilated cattle this morning. She got up and went to the door. With the blinds pulled across the window, she couldn't see who stood on the other side. She wasn't about to open the door until she knew who it was. Before she opened it, she grabbed the cord and pulled up the blinds.

She gasped in horror at the sight of a man wearing a ski mask on the other side. She stumbled backward as the man picked up an ax and slammed it into the door, shattering the glass and cracking the wood.

For a long moment, she stood frozen in horror. When he raised the ax and hit the door once again, she screamed and sprang into action. She whirled around and raced for her room.

The crack of wood splintering sounded again, and she knew she only had seconds before the man would be in her house. She flew down the dark hallway and into her bedroom, frantic to get to her shotgun, which was locked up in a gun case in her closet.

The continuing sound of cracking wood let her know the man wouldn't stop attacking the door until he got inside. Terrified tears raced down her cheeks as she fumbled to get the gun. She finally got the case open and grabbed the shotgun. Once she had it in her hands, she gripped it tightly and peeked out of her bedroom.

Silence.

It pressed in and made her chest tighten and her heart race so quickly she thought she might have a heart attack. The silence meant the man was now in the house.

At the moment she didn't care who he was—she was going to shoot first and ask questions later. He was in here to hurt her...to potentially kill her. She didn't intend to give him the chance.

He'd apparently been watching her house. He must have seen Jake and Andy leave and knew she'd be in here alone and vulnerable. Once again she tightened her grip on the gun. Using it to lead the way, she took a step out of her bedroom.

She stopped and tried to listen to any noise she might hear that would indicate where the man was now. It was difficult to hear over the pounding of her heart and the frantic gasps of fear that escaped her mouth.

Nothing. She heard nothing, and not knowing where he was made her fear ratchet up even higher. She tried to silence her own gasps and frantic breaths, knowing he would be able to track her by the sounds she made.

She took another step and then another. She was about to peek into the bathroom when he reached out of the darkness of that room and, despite her tight grip, snatched her gun away from her. He threw the gun behind him in the bathroom as she screamed.

"Who are you? What do you want?" she shrieked. "Why? Why are you doing this to me?"

There was no way to run around him in the narrow hallway, and before she could turn to run back into her bedroom, he grabbed her around the neck. He pushed until her back was against the wall next to the bathroom doorway.

His eyes were dark, glittering orbs of evil as he began to squeeze her throat. Tighter…tighter he squeezed. Her fingers scrabbled at his hands in an effort to dislodge them as her oxygen was slowly cut off.

Stars flickered, and then her vision dimmed as no more air reached her lungs…her brain. She was going to die. Jake would come home and find her dead body. And what would happen to Andy?

It was the thought of her son that gave her the strength for one more effort to survive. As her beloved son's face filled her head, she drew up a knee and slammed it between his legs as hard as she could.

Instantly he groaned, released his grip on her and fell to his knees. She ran into the living room, knowing her best option was to try to hide until Jake got back.

A roar of rage sounded from the hallway. "I'm going to kill you, bitch," he cried.

The voice was unfamiliar to her. Who was the man and why was he doing this to her? Knowing the house would be a death trap to remain in, Eva flew out the front door, hoping and praying she could somehow survive until Jake got home.

As Jake drove toward town, evidence of storm damage from the night before was visible in the amount of tree limbs and branches that were down around the area.

"Wow, look at that one," Andy said and pointed to a big limb on the ground almost encroaching onto the other lane in the road. "Must have been a big storm, and I didn't even know it was happening."

"It was mostly just a lot of wind and rain," Jake replied. "Trust me, it was worth sleeping through."

"But you stayed awake with Mom?" he asked.

"I did. She wanted to keep an eye on the weather so she could keep you safe and sound."

"We had to go to the storm cellar one time when I was seven," Andy said. "But nothing happened and we were only down there for a little while."

"That's good," Jake replied.

"You like my mom, don't you, Mr. Jake?"

Jake felt the boy's attention riveted to him. "Of course I like your mom," Jake replied. "What's not to like? She's beautiful and smart and funny."

"But you *like* like her, don't you?"

"Yes, I *like* like her."

"I thought so," Andy replied with a look of self-satisfaction.

Jake was grateful to pull up in front of the school to stop any more questions Andy might have about him and his mother's relationship. It wasn't his place to talk about these things with Andy.

Jake found a parking place, and the two of them got out. He walked Andy to the school's front door. "Have a great day, Andy."

"I will, and thanks for bringing me, Mr. Jake." Andy quickly headed for the door and disappeared into the building, and Jake turned around to head back to his truck.

Before he got there, he ran into Benny, who carried a colorful lunchbox in his hand. "Hey, Jake," Benny greeted him. "I'm here because boy child left his lunch at home. What are you doing here?"

"I brought Eva's son to school," Jake replied.

"I heard that you were spending a lot of time with her. I've also heard there's some messed-up stuff going on at her ranch."

"Yeah, there is," Jake admitted.

"We still need to plan that dinner. I'd love to have not only you, but Eva and her son as well."

"That would be great, and we'll plan something soon, but right now I've got to get back to Eva's."

"I'm definitely going to call you soon to set up a dinner at our house," Benny said.

"I look forward to it. I'll talk to you later, Benny." Jake hurried back to his truck and headed for home.

He was eager to get back to Eva. Last night he'd felt a new emotional connection growing between them. They had talked about so many things that had nothing to do with who they had been as teenagers and everything to do with who they were as adults. He'd never felt as close to her as he did right now after the long night they had shared.

He couldn't believe how he'd overslept. He hadn't slept that late since he'd been a kid. He frowned as he looked ahead. The road was blocked by a city truck removing the large tree limb that Andy had pointed out earlier.

He came to a stop behind several other cars. There was no other route to get to Eva's ranch, and so he was stuck. Hopefully they'd get the big branch moved quickly and he could be on his way.

Already he was aware of the time ticking by. He told himself Eva would be fine. It was a morning filled with sunshine, surely not the time for any evil to take place.

Sometimes bad things happen in the light of day, a little voice whispered in the back of his head. He mentally shook his head to dislodge the thought.

There was no way anyone could have known that he and Eva would oversleep this morning and he'd end up taking Andy to school, leaving Eva alone in her house. Besides, she had good locks on the doors and windows and a gun she could get to if necessary.

He tapped his fingers impatiently on the steering wheel as he continued to be held up. He glanced in his rearview mirror and saw a line of cars now behind him.

He pulled out his phone and dialed Eva's number. He needed to tell her he was held up so she wouldn't worry. The phone rang three times and then went to voice mail.

He hung up without leaving a message. Maybe she was in the shower or her phone was still in the bedroom and she was in the kitchen and couldn't hear it. He waited five minutes and then tried to call her again. Same result…the call went to voice mail.

He tried to ignore the small bell of alarm that began to ring in his head. There could be all kinds of reasons she wasn't answering her phone. It didn't mean that she was in any kind of trouble.

Still, he needed to get back to her as soon as possible, if nothing else to still the faint alarm still ringing in his head. Finally the branch was removed, and the traffic began to move again. He stepped on the gas and drove as quickly as possible.

When he reached Eva's place, he was relieved to see nothing amiss. He parked and then hurried to the front door. It was locked. "Eva," he yelled and banged on the door. He waited a moment, and when she didn't reply, he took out the key she had given him a week before and unlocked the door.

He walked in and called her name once again. She didn't answer. He yelled her name louder, and the alarm bell in his head rang a little louder when she still didn't reply. The shower wasn't running, so she wasn't in the bathroom unable to hear him.

He flipped on the light and stared down the hallway but stopped and froze. Just inside the doorway of the bathroom, Eva's shotgun was on the floor. Immediately every muscle in his body tightened, and adrenaline fired through his veins. Where was Eva now? Why was her shotgun on the floor? Oh God, what had happened here while he'd been gone?

He hurried into the kitchen and stopped short as

he stared at what was left of the back door. Shattered glass littered the floor, and the wood of the door had been completely splintered apart, making a hole large enough for somebody to enter the house.

He ran to the door and peered outside. His heart iced as he saw the ax that had apparently been used to break in. Where was Eva? At least he hadn't found her dead body lying on the floor...at least not in the kitchen.

With his heart in his throat, he turned back and raced toward Andy's room. *Please, please don't let me find her dead*, he prayed. He released a small sigh of relief when he didn't find her in her son's room. He then ran toward her room and once again prayed that he wouldn't find her lifeless in the bed or on the floor.

She wasn't on the floor on this side of the king-size bed, but what about the other side? He hurried around the foot of the bed. A gasp of relief swept over him when she wasn't there.

Not finding her anywhere in the house, he returned to the kitchen. Stepping outside, his heart thundered a million miles a minute, and he pulled his gun from his holster. He gazed around and listened, hoping to hear something...anything that would let him know where she was and that she was still alive.

Nothing. All he heard were birds singing in the trees and a cow mooing in the pasture. They were normal sounds, daytime noises, but the lack of any other noises scared him half to death.

His heart squeezed so tight he could scarcely draw a breath. Was he too late? Had he taken so long to get home that Eva had been killed? Was her body right now lying someplace in a pasture? Hidden in one of the outbuildings?

"Eva?" he yelled as loud as he could. Nothing. There was nothing to let him know whether she was dead or alive, but the silence cut deeply into his heart.

He had to do something to find her. If she'd run from the house, then maybe she was in one of the outbuildings. Maybe she'd somehow locked herself inside and now was afraid to come out.

With his gun still tightly gripped in his hand, he took off running toward the shed in the distance. He could only hope and pray that he would find her alive somewhere, because the alternative was too horrendous to consider.

EVA LEFT THE HOUSE and ran hell-bent toward the barn, hoping she could hide in there until Jake got home, hoping she could get inside before the man who was after her saw where she went.

She raced as fast as she could, her heart beating so hard…so fast…it felt as if it might explode out of her chest. She couldn't believe this was happening. Her nightmares were coming true, and she knew if the man caught her, he intended to kill her.

Why? The question screamed over and over again in her brain. Why was this happening? Why was a monster breaking into her home and trying to kill her? Who was the monster behind the ski mask?

She reached the barn, threw the door open and raced across the floor. When she came to the ladder, she climbed up as quickly as she could into the loft. She wanted to hide in the farthest corner of the building.

She found a stack of hay with a small space between it and the wall, and she quickly crawled in. She shoved her hand in her mouth to stop the hysterical cries that escaped her. Terrified tears chased fast and furious down her cheeks.

It was only when she was hunkered down that she realized she had put herself in a place without an exit. If he found her here, there was now positively nowhere for her to run. She could throw herself out the loft door, but the fall would probably kill her.

Quiet as a mouse. That's what she needed to be right now. *Quiet as a mouse,* she told herself over and over again. She nearly screamed as the barn door flew open. "I know you're in here, Eva. Come on out now." He laughed, the sound holding a maniacal glee that caused arctic chills to race up and down Eva's back.

She didn't recognize the low, raspy voice and suspected he was intentionally trying to disguise it from her. Did he really know for a fact she was in here hiding, or was he bluffing?

Once again she placed her hand over her mouth,

fear welling up in the back of her throat and begging to be released on a hysterical scream.

Quiet as a mouse, she thought again. If he wasn't sure that she was in here, maybe if he heard nothing he'd go check out someplace else. *Please, go away*, she begged in her mind. *Please, please just go away.*

"Come on, Eva. You might as well give it up now. I'm going to search every inch of this barn, and I will find you and then I'm going to kill you." She heard what sounded like a stack of hay bales falling over and hitting the ground.

Where was Jake? What was taking him so long to get back from the school? Surely he should be home by now. It felt as if he'd been gone for hours. If he didn't get back soon, the man was going to find her, and even though she'd fight with all her heart and soul, she knew eventually he would be able to overpower her.

Again a question shot through her mind. Not the why of what was happening, but rather what would become of Andy if she was killed.

As it stood right now, he'd probably wind up in foster care, and the very idea of that happening was excruciating. She should have told Jake the truth. She should have told him that Andy was his son the minute he'd arrived back in Dusty Gulch. If she somehow survived this, she would tell Jake and take whatever consequences might happen.

Of course what she hoped was, even without Jake knowing the truth, he would petition the courts to have Andy in his custody. At least she'd know Andy would be raised with Jake's love. She no longer worried about Jake being tainted by his family's wealth and power. Jake's heart was as pure as it had been when he'd been a teenager, and she couldn't imagine that ever changing. But first, she had to survive.

"Eva, are you up here?"

She heard him take a heavy step on the ladder leading to the loft. "You must be up here, because I saw you run into the barn and I've checked all around down here. The longer I have to look for you, the angrier I'm becoming."

Another footstep sounded on the loft stairs. Terror tensed every muscle in her body with a fight-or-flight adrenaline. There was no place for her to take flight to, but she intended to fight until there was no more fight left in her body.

"You should have just left town, Eva. Things would have been so much better for you if you had just picked up and moved to another state when I first warned you."

She only hoped before she died, she saw the face of the monster beneath the ski mask. Maybe it would help her understand why, exactly, he wanted her dead.

She knew when he had reached the loft, because she could now hear his excited, rapid breathing. Could he hear her? Oh God, where on earth was Jake?

Hay bales began to topple down on the other side of the hayloft. If he was on the other side of the loft, then maybe she could get to the loft stairway before he could and she could get away. She had to do something or he would find her. Backed against the wall, there would be no way for her to get away from him.

She drew in several silent deep breaths and then sprang up and ran for the stairs. She almost made it, but he caught her by the ends of her long hair. He spun her around and to the floor as she screamed... and screamed...and screamed.

He was on top of her in an instant, his hands encircling her neck. "Who are you?" she gasped as his thumbs began pressing hard into her throat.

"You'll never know," he replied.

Her hands reached up in a frantic effort to dislodge his, but he was too strong. He was on top of her in a way that trapped her legs so there was no way she could bring up a knee in order to hit him where it might count.

This was it. She was going to die in this place where she had once found love. She would never see Jake again. Worse, she would never see Andy's smile again or hear his laughter.

Tears wept from the sides of her eyes as her air disappeared. Her lungs began to burn. Stars exploded in her brain. Her vision dimmed.

She was just about to lose total consciousness when she heard a distant roar and the man on top of her was suddenly gone. She rolled over to her side, gasping and coughing for air.

She opened her eyes just in time to see Jake hit

the man once…twice…three times so hard in the jaw, the man fell backward and onto the floor. Jake immediately leaned down and held his gun at the man's temple. He pulled back on the hammer.

"No, Jake," she said between coughs. "Don't kill him."

"I want to." Jake's voice shook with his rage. "I want to kill him for hurting you, but I won't." He released the hammer without shooting but kept his gun pointed at the intruder.

"Get up before I change my mind." He reached down and yanked the man up by the front of his black shirt.

Jake pulled his phone out of his back pocket and slid it across the floor to where Eva had sat up. "Eva, honey, call Wayne. We need to get this scum arrested and put away."

As Jake continued to hold the man at gunpoint, Eva called Wayne. "Sheriff Black," he answered on the second ring.

"Wayne, it's Eva. We have him." A sob of deep relief choked out of her. "He tried to kill me, but Jake has him and we need you to come out. We're in the barn loft."

"I'm on my way," Wayne replied.

Eva hung up the phone and stared at the masked man who had just tried to take her life. There was no doubt that he was the same man who had mutilated her cattle and hung the bloody heart on her railing.

He was the same man who had attacked her in the barn and had put fear in her son's eyes.

"I need to know… I need to know who he is," Eva said. "Pull his mask off."

Jake reached out for the bottom of the ski mask, but the man pulled back from him. "I'll pull that off you dead or alive," Jake said angrily. He reached out once again and this time yanked off the ski mask.

Eva gasped in stunned surprise as she finally saw the face of her monster.

Chapter Thirteen

"David?" The very earth seemed to move beneath Jake's feet as he stared at his brother. Confusion weighed heavy in Jake's mind. Of all the people he'd expected to see, his brother was the very last. It didn't make sense. "You? It's been you behind all this?"

"I did it for you, Jake," David said. "Come on, man. She's nothing. She's nobody. I was just trying to protect you."

"Protect me?" Jake continued to stare at his brother in stunned shock. "Protect me from what?"

David looked down at his feet and then back at Jake. "I guess I haven't been thinking clearly since Dad's death."

"You mutilated the first cow weeks before your father's death," Eva said.

David frowned and didn't even acknowledge Eva's presence with a glance in her direction. His dark gaze bored into Jake's. "Jake, why don't you just let me walk away from all this and we all can just forget what has happened?"

"Forget that you terrorized me for over two months?" Eva got to her feet and moved to stand next to Jake. Her voice was husky and her throat was red and bruised, threatening to make Jake's anger rise up once again.

"Forget that you just tried to kill me?" Eva's voice shook with emotion. "That if Jake hadn't gotten here in time you would have succeeded?"

"Jake, just shoot her and let's get out of here," David said. "Come on, brother. Do the right thing. I'm your family."

"Do the right thing? What in the hell is wrong with you?" Jake pulled Eva close against his side. "The right thing is you are going to be arrested, and you're going to prison for a very long time."

David's eyes narrowed. "I gave her a chance to leave town. She should have heeded my warnings. She's bad, Jake. She's always been bad. She's ruinous for you, and you should have nothing to do with her. She's poison."

"Is that why you did all this?" Jake was still trying to wrap his head around the fact that his brother was behind all the attacks, that his brother had just tried to kill Eva.

David's face grew red with rage. "Don't you get it, Jake? Even Dad knew she was no good for you, that she didn't deserve to be anywhere around an Albright. And speaking of dear old Dad, while you were whooping it up in Italy, I was the one who had to suffer his foul moods and coldness. I was the one he mentally and verbally abused on a daily basis."

"I'm sorry for that, David," Jake replied. "But that doesn't excuse what you've done."

"You always defended Dad. You always tried to brownnose him, but he hated you as much as he hated me. He should have been sterile and never allowed to have children."

David's eyes glittered with utter hatred, and Jake couldn't believe the kind of vitriol that had been inside his brother. "But you loved dear old Dad," he continued. "Maybe you wouldn't have loved him so much if you'd known that he was behind Eva breaking up with you all those years ago."

Jake frowned and looked at Eva just in time to see all the color leave her face. "What's he talking about, Eva?"

"We can talk about it later," she replied. "Wayne should be here anytime. Maybe we should get down from the loft."

Although Jake wanted to ask her about what David had said, he knew there would be time to talk to her after David was officially arrested.

"Eva, you go on down and then we'll follow," Jake instructed. He was still in shock that the person behind everything wasn't Griff or Robert, but rather his own brother. And he still didn't understand David's reasoning for wanting Eva dead. There had to be more to it than David somehow trying to protect Jake from her.

"Just let me go before Wayne gets here," David said as soon as Eva had left the loft. "You can tell him the man escaped and you never pulled off his ski mask. You can tell Wayne you still don't know who the perp is."

"And what about Eva?"

"Tell Wayne she's lying about me. It would be your word against hers, and Wayne would believe an Albright over a poor piece of trash like Eva."

Once again Jake looked at David as if he were a stranger—a very disturbed stranger. When he thought of David cutting the heart out of a cow, his brain threatened to explode. Who would have thought David had such evil inside him?

"Head downstairs," he said. "And David, if you try to get away, I'll shoot you in the leg. Don't test me, because I promise you I'll shoot."

When they reached the main level of the barn, Eva waited for them, her face still pale and her throat a livid red that already had taken on shades of deep purple.

Jake's chest tightened with a rage of his own. How dare David put a finger on the woman Jake loved? How dare he fill her life with the kind of fear Eva had experienced?

David must think Jake was totally crazy if he thought Jake was going to just let him go and forget all this. As much as he loved his brother, David had to go to jail and pay the consequences for what he had done.

At that moment Wayne and a couple of his deputies walked through the barn door. Wayne looked as surprised as anyone to see David.

"What's going on here?" he asked.

"David tried to kill me," Eva said, and a hand went to her throat. "He...he tried to strangle me." Tears filled her eyes, along with a look of residual fear. "He's behind it all, Wayne. He did it all. He killed my cattle and hung the heart, and this morning he broke through my back door with an ax and...and I managed to escape him, but I ran to the loft and then he tried to kill me by strangling me to death."

The words rushed out of her as tears chased down her cheeks. Once again Jake pulled her against his side. "Whoa," Wayne said. "We need to slow things down."

"I just want him arrested. I...I don't ever want to see him again." Eva turned her face into Jake's chest.

"Wayne, they're both crazy," David said. "You know me. I'm an Albright, and if you put me under arrest, I can promise you that you'll be sorry."

"David, we've always gotten along, but I'm the law. I really don't give a damn if you're an Albright or the governor of this state. If you broke the law, then you have to pay the consequences." He nodded at the two deputies with him.

They placed David in handcuffs, and David exploded in rage. "Why didn't you just die?" he screamed at Eva. "My son is a real Albright, and he's not going to share his inheritance with your bastard son or any children you might have. You aren't Albright material—you're nothing but trash."

Jake frowned. Bastard son? What was he talking about? He looked at Eva. He hadn't thought it was possible, but her face was now even whiter than it had been. Shock tried to work through him, but he fought against it. Surely David was mistaken in his thinking. He looked back at his brother. "Share an inheritance? So this was all about money?"

"Of course that's what it was about," David screamed, his face red and spittle flying. "It's about money and power and keeping it where it belongs, with the rightful Albrights. Dad knew she was trash, and that's why he got her to break up with you. But the minute you got back to town, you ran back to her like a dog in heat. I had to do something... I had to protect you from yourself."

"Take him away," Jake said in disgust. He couldn't trust anything David was telling him. It was obvious his brother was deeply disturbed.

"I'll need full statements from the two of you," Wayne said once David had been led out of the barn by the two deputies. "Are you up to giving them to me now?"

"I want to get this behind me as soon as possible," Eva said wearily. "So, let's do it and get it done."

They walked back to her house in silence. Jake's brain tried to sort out everything that had happened, everything that had been said, but he was still in a numbing shock that it had been David who had committed all the crimes.

A glance at Eva let him know she was probably in the same mental space. Her face was still pale, and as she reached up to shove a strand of hair behind her ear, her fingers trembled.

They went through the front door, and Eva led Wayne into the kitchen. "I'll be right back." She left the room.

The sight of what was left of the splintered back door still shocked Jake. He couldn't imagine the kind of terror that had to have filled Eva while David was breaking in with an ax.

"Hell of a mess," Wayne said when Eva had left the kitchen. "I would have never suspected David."

"I'm still in complete shock," Jake admitted. "He was behind it all, Wayne. My own brother was killing cattle and tormenting Eva. My own brother tried to kill her."

Eva came back into the kitchen wearing a robe over the thin nightgown she'd had on. She grabbed a broom from the pantry and began sweeping up the broken glass that littered the floor.

Wayne and Jake watched her for a minute or two. "Eva, come sit down," Wayne finally said. "I need your full attention while you're giving me your statement."

"I'll help you clean up later," Jake said gently. "Come sit down and let's get this over with." She hesitated a moment and then returned the broom to the pantry and joined them at the table.

"Do either of you mind if I tape this?" Wayne asked. They both said no, and Wayne pulled a small tape recorder out of his pocket. He set it on the table, spoke into it with the time and date, and then looked at Eva. "Tell me what happened this morning from the very beginning."

Her voice shook as she explained to Wayne about them oversleeping and Jake taking Andy to school. "When they were gone, I sat right here at the table and drank a cup of coffee, and then I started to leave the kitchen to get dressed for the day. I saw a person's shadow at the back door, and I assumed it must be Harley. I wasn't going to open the door until I was sure. So, I pulled up the blinds, and that's when I saw him."

The color that had crept back into her face faded once again. Jake reached over and captured her hand with his. Her fingers tightly squeezed his. "He had an ax, and he started hitting the door."

Her voice became breathless as she told them about running for her gun and then David knocking the weapon out of her hands. She recounted him choking her in the hallway and her hitting him to get away.

"I ran to the barn and climbed into the loft, hoping and praying I could hide from him until Jake got back home. He almost killed me... I was about to lose consciousness when Jake showed up."

"I got home and couldn't find her," Jake said. "When I saw the back door and didn't find her anywhere in the house, I knew she must have run outside, but I had no idea where she might be."

This time it was his fingers that squeezed hers. "I heard her scream and ran into the barn and realized she was up in the loft. I got up there and saw a man on top of her and strangling her." Even now, knowing she was safe, his chest still tightened as he remembered that moment.

"I pulled him off her and punched him and then pulled my gun. I wanted to shoot him, Wayne. I wanted to kill him for what he'd done to Eva. I can't believe it was David the whole time. I still can't believe it."

"He wasn't even on a long list of suspects," Wayne replied. "If he hadn't been caught in the act, we probably would have never caught him."

As Wayne and Eva continued to talk, Jake still tried to process that his brother had been behind everything, that David had actually tried to kill Eva. It was still difficult for him to comprehend.

It was just after noon when Wayne and his men finished photographing and collecting evidence both in the house and in the barn.

While Eva went into the bedroom to get out of her robe and nightgown and into clothes, Jake sat on the sofa to wait for her.

They still needed to clean up the kitchen where the door had been broken down, and they would need to contact somebody about a replacement door. But before any of that could happen, Jake needed some answers from her.

More than anything, he needed to know once and for all exactly what had happened ten years ago.

EVEN THOUGH EVA knew Jake was waiting for her, she took a hot shower before she got dressed. She needed to wash away the feel of David's hands on her, the abject evil she felt had touched her.

She had already had a showdown with a killer, and she suspected she was about to have one with Jake even though she didn't physically or mentally feel like having any more conflict for the day.

But David had opened up a whole can of worms, and she knew the time had come to pay for her past sins. When this was all over, she'd be alone, and she tried to tell herself that was what she'd wanted all along, but she couldn't help the weight of sadness that rode her shoulders as she went back into the living room.

She eased down on the sofa next to him. Her throat still burned and hurt, and now that the adrenaline of the moment had worn off, she had aches and pains in other areas of her body from the fight for her life.

"Eva." Jake reached out and took her hands in his, his beautiful eyes radiating pain. "I'm so sorry."

She looked at him in surprise. "What are you sorry about?"

The pain in his eyes deepened. "It was my own brother who did all these things to you. My brother..." He shook his head.

"Jake, you aren't responsible for your brother's actions," she replied softly.

He released her hands and instead raced his hands through his thick hair. "I know, but somehow I should have sensed something was off with him. I should have seen this coming."

"How could you? Why would either one of us even consider David wanting to harm me? I didn't even know your brother personally. This had nothing to do with you, Jake, so don't try to take any responsibility for it."

"Thank God I got here in time," he said.

She raised a hand to her throat, remembering that moment when she'd been positive she was going to die. "If you'd been one minute longer, I would have been gone. He would have succeeded in killing me."

He held her gaze for a long moment. "Eva, tell me what happened ten years ago. Why did you break up with me and what part did my father play in all of it?"

She'd never expected this moment to come, when she'd have to talk to him about all this. He'd just had his brother exposed as a killer, and she hated to tell him now anything about his father that would destroy Jake's image of the man.

But it was time for truth telling. Before he left here today, he would know all her secrets, and she feared the consequences that would affect the rest of her life.

"Eva, it's time for us to talk about the past," he said.

"I know." She broke eye contact with him and instead looked down at the coffee table. "The night before I broke up with you, I was in the barn feeding the horses some treats when your father showed up."

She remembered how shocked she'd been to see Justin Albright parked in front of her home. He had been a tall, imposing man with cold, dark eyes. "I invited him inside, but he refused to come in and told me he just wanted to talk to me."

"What did he have to say?" Jake's voice was filled with tension, the same kind of tension that now twisted her stomach as she looked at him once again.

"He told me if I didn't stop seeing you, then he'd destroy my father. He would see to it that he lost the ranch and wound up with nothing." Jake's eyes filled with a new pain.

"Jake, if he'd threatened me, I probably wouldn't have broken up with you, but I couldn't risk him hurting my father. I knew he had the power to do what he threatened, and I was so afraid, so the next night I broke up with you. It was the most difficult thing I've ever done in my life. I'm sorry, Jake."

A new pain slashed across his features. "Don't apologize. I think somehow in the back of my mind I always wondered if he'd been involved in your decision to not see me anymore."

He leaned forward and raked his hands through his hair once again. "My family has caused nothing but pain in your life, Eva." He straightened up. "Why didn't you tell me at the time what my father had done?"

"Oh Jake, I knew how much you loved your father. The last thing I wanted to do was take that away from you. In any case, even if I told you, your father still held all the power."

"It all just makes me so sad." His gaze softened as he looked at her. "I was so in love with you, Eva. If my father hadn't interfered, I believe we would have gotten married and been happy for the rest of our lives."

"I believe the same thing, but he did interfere and that didn't happen," she replied softly.

They were silent for a moment, and all Eva could think about was the bombshell secret she still had to confess to him. She was vaguely surprised he hadn't already figured it out from what David had said about inheritances. However, the shock of finding out it was his own brother behind her terror might have made him miss a lot of what David had actually said.

She suddenly realized how much she wanted Jake to love her as he had before his father had gotten involved. She wanted him to love her for the rest of his life, as she knew she would love him. But she feared her final confession would send him out of her life, and he would leave behind utter devastation.

"Let me tell you what happened after I broke up with you and you went to Italy." She got up from the sofa, unable to sit next to him and tell him the depth of her deception.

She pulled the shade on the window, letting in the sunshine, and then turned to face him. "You'd been gone about two and a half weeks when my father died. Needless to say, I was devastated, and that's when Andrew stepped up as a comfort to me. I was overwhelmed with so many things, and he's the one who taught me what I needed to do to keep the ranch running smoothly."

"I wish it had been me, Eva," Jake said softly.

She nodded and smiled. "I know." Her smile lasted only a moment. "Anyway, Andrew came to me with the idea of an arrangement. He already knew he was dying. He hadn't been given that long to live, but he didn't want to die alone in a hospital surrounded by strangers. So, I agreed to marry him and take care of him to the end."

Jake frowned. "But if it was an arrangement, then what was in it for you? Were you in love with Andrew?"

"I came to love him in the three years we had together, but no, I didn't marry him for love. I agreed to marry him because he would give my unborn baby a name. I was pregnant, Jake. I was pregnant with your baby when I broke up with you."

"Andy is my son?"

She nodded and held her breath as he stared at her.

The softness she'd seen shining from his eyes cooled and then hardened. "You should have told me, Eva. If you really wanted to, you could have figured out a way to get in touch with me in Italy."

"I was afraid, Jake. I was so afraid that if your father found out I was pregnant with your child, he would figure out a way to get the baby taken away from me and he'd follow through on his threat to destroy my father," she replied.

He stood, his eyes dark and unfathomable. "Why didn't you tell me when I got back here? My father was dead. Why didn't you tell me then?"

He didn't wait for a response from her. "You had no right, Eva. You had no right to keep him away from me. Nine years... I've lost nine years of his life, Eva." Anger tightened his features. "I've got to get out of here." He headed for the front door.

"Jake...wait," she protested. "Please, let's talk."

"Right now I'm too angry to talk." He opened the door and stalked outside.

Eva fought the impulse to run after him, to throw her arms around his neck and beg him to forgive her. But she didn't. Instead she sank down on the sofa and began to weep.

It had been her cowardice that had kept her silent when she'd first realized she was pregnant. She'd been a coward again when she hadn't told him about his son when he'd shown back up in town.

Jake had been betrayed today first by his brother, then by his father and finally by the woman he loved.

While her heart ached for him, her tears were also for herself.

She'd been devastated when she'd lost Jake's love the first time, and she realized it was very possible she'd just lost it for a second time.

She'd survived the attack by David, but she wasn't at all sure she'd survive what might happen in her future where Jake and Andy were concerned.

Chapter Fourteen

Jake felt as if his very heart had been ripped out of his chest. He drove aimlessly as his chaotic thoughts tried to find some sense of order in his brain.

He'd thought David was just spewing out some kind of delusional nonsense when he'd talked about his son sharing his inheritance. He'd believed David was worried that he and Eva might have a child together in the future. He hadn't thought about Andy.

He was thrilled that the bright, loving boy was his own, but right now his heart was too bruised and battered by the fact that he'd lost so many years with Andy.

He'd missed not only the birth, but the first word...first step...a million other firsts that had already occurred. It was all time he could never get back.

She should have contacted him the minute she'd realized she was pregnant. Somehow, someway, they would have figured something out. But she obviously hadn't trusted him enough to be able to stand up to his father. He would have stood up to the devil himself if it meant staying with Eva and his son.

He wasn't sure whether he wanted to rage or to weep at all the overwhelming events of the day. He drove back country roads for the next hour or so and finally wound up at the Albright mansion.

His head was no clearer, but he was exhausted by all the emotional turmoil. It wasn't until he parked out front that he suddenly thought about his sister-in-law. Oh God, had Stephanie heard about what had happened?

Had she known what her husband was up to? No, there was no way Jake believed Stephanie would have any part in harming another human being. There was no way anything like that was in her DNA.

He walked into the hallway and called her name. She came out of the sitting room and stood frozen in the doorway. Her eyes were swollen and red-rimmed, and he instantly knew that she had heard what had happened.

"Ah, Steph," he said softly and opened his arms to her. She walked into his embrace and cried into his shoulder for several minutes. She finally stepped back from him and swiped her cheeks.

He took her by the hand and led her to the sofa in the sitting room where he pulled her down to sit next to him. "How did you hear?"

"Wayne stopped by to question me. I…Jake… I had no idea." Tears once again filled her eyes. "I knew something was going on with him. David was gone almost all the time. He left here early in the morning and didn't return until the middle of the night.

"He told me he was working on some new contracts, that it was business that had him staying gone all the time. But normally he did his work here in the office. He told me he was spending his time in his office in town, but I drove by there one night and he wasn't there."

She released a short, half-hysterical laugh as more tears spilled from her eyes. "He'd become so secretive and distant, I suspected he was having an affair. God, I wish it had been an affair. What he did...what he tried to do was absolutely unspeakable."

Her eyes became haunted. "I knew there were times David could be ruthless in his business dealings. I also knew he could have a cruel streak with the way he sometimes spoke to me, but even I wasn't aware of the utter evil he had inside him. I'm so sorry, Jake. And please tell Eva how sorry I am."

"I'm not sure how long it will be before I'm ready to speak to Eva again," he replied, his heart aching once again.

"What do you mean?"

Jake told Stephanie about everything he'd learned from Eva...about his father's machinations to keep the young lovers apart and about Jake being Andy's father.

"Nine years, Stephanie. I've missed nine years of

Andy's life because Eva kept this secret from me." Anger swept through him once again.

"I'm so sorry, Jake," Stephanie said. "So, what are you going to do now?"

"To be honest, I don't know," he confessed. "I'm too angry right now to make any kind of a decision."

"I hope whatever you decide to do, you'll be kind to Eva. She must have been so afraid that your father would find out, and in any case, hasn't the Albright family done enough damage to her?" Stephanie stood. "And now I've got some packing to do. If you could give me just a couple of days, then I'll be out of here."

Jake looked at her in surprise. "Out of here? Stephanie, this is your home. Why would you pack up and leave?"

Her eyes became red and glassy with impending tears. "I was here because I was married to your brother, and now I intend to seek a divorce from him and he'll be in prison for years to come. I have no place here anymore."

"That's nonsense. You are still my sister-in-law, and Richard is still my nephew. You're my family, and you're welcome to live here for as long as you want."

"Are you sure?" Tears filled her eyes once again and escaped down her cheeks.

"I'm very sure," Jake replied firmly.

"Thank you, Jake. I was feeling so lost. I was feeling like I'd not only lost my husband but also my home. I've been in a haze since Wayne left."

"Well, you don't have to worry about losing your home. You and Richard will always have a place here." Jake stood and so did Steph.

She hugged Jake and then stepped back, tears chasing down her cheeks once again. "I still can't believe what David did. I wish I could have some-way stopped him, but I just didn't see the evil and hatred he had in his heart for Eva."

"Don't beat yourself up, Steph. None of us saw this coming."

She nodded. "Richard is taking a nap. I think maybe I'll rest a bit."

"That's exactly what I plan on doing right now."

Together they walked up the staircase. "Jake, I hope you find forgiveness in your heart for Eva. She's been a victim in this for a long time." She didn't wait for his reply, but instead turned and headed down the hallway toward her suite of rooms.

Jake released a deep sigh and headed for his own rooms. He couldn't imagine what Stephanie was going through right now. Her entire world had been destroyed by the man she'd loved and trusted, by the man who was the father of her son.

He slumped down on the sofa in his sitting room, his thoughts still in chaos where Eva was concerned. He wanted to hate her for what she'd done. He wanted to despise her for keeping Andy a secret for so many years.

But there was a more rational part of his brain that understood the choices she'd made. Certainly he now understood why she had broken up with him on that night so long ago.

Eva would have done anything to protect her father, and Jake knew how frightening his father could be. Eva had loved her father, and the threat against him must have been terrifying for her. Jake had adored his father, but now he realized he'd adored a man who didn't exist.

Justin Albright had been a bully who used his power and money to bend people to his will. God knew how many victims Justin had left behind when he'd died. He'd used his power and money against his own son, to destroy Jake's dream of marrying Eva and living the life of a simple rancher.

He tried to imagine how Eva must have felt when she'd been eighteen years old. Her father had died unexpectedly, and she'd discovered she was pregnant by a man who lived in Italy and at that time had hated her for breaking up with him.

She must have been absolutely terrified. She could have decided not to have the baby. Thankfully she hadn't made that choice. She'd chosen to have his baby despite the odds stacked against her.

He also wanted to hate Andrew Martin, but he couldn't hate the man who had helped Eva survive, the man who had agreed to give his son his name. He couldn't hate the man who had loved Andy for three years before his death. In fact, he thanked God that Andrew had been there for Eva.

Jake got up and began to pace, trying to untangle

his emotions. There was no question that he now wanted plenty of quality time with his son.

Andy should be home from school now. Had Eva told him? If she hadn't yet, then when did she intend to tell him the truth? He had a feeling Andy would be thrilled to have a real, living and breathing father to add to his life. And Jake was positive Andy would be happy to discover that man was Jake.

In the time Jake had spent at Eva's, he and Andy had completely bonded. Jake had fallen in love with Andy even when he'd believed he wasn't Andy's father.

All he had to figure out now was exactly how or if he intended to coparent with Eva.

EVA SANK DOWN on her sofa and listened to the silence around her. It was the first time in weeks she didn't have the simmering fear as a companion. David Albright was in jail, and her back door had been repaired.

There would be no more dead cattle or chilling notes. She didn't have to worry about anyone wanting to kill her anymore. The danger was gone, and she should feel deliriously happy.

But she didn't. All she felt was a deep sadness and a new kind of fear. She hadn't told Andy the truth about Jake yet. Andy was now sleeping peacefully in bed, unaware of how his life was going to change.

And it was that change that now frightened her. She had no idea what Jake was going to do about

Andy. Would he fight her for full custody because she had had Andy to herself for the past nine years?

She couldn't imagine not tucking her son into bed at night or seeing his bright morning smile. It was torturous to think that she wouldn't hear about Andy's school adventures the minute he got off the bus, or they wouldn't deliver his eggs together.

And the worst thing of all was that without the danger, without the fear, she was left with only her love for Jake. It had always been him in her heart.

The teenage boy who had sat barefoot on the dock next to her had become the man she wished to spend the rest of her life with. But she didn't believe that would happen now.

In the end Justin Albright had won and the two young lovers would never, ever find happily-ever-after with each other.

Tears filled her eyes, but she quickly swiped them away. Maybe she'd cry later. What had happened with Jake was her own fault. She'd kept the secret of Andy too long, and now she could only wonder what price she'd have to pay.

Maybe she should just go to bed. She'd already put on her nightgown, and exhaustion weighed heavily on her. She could escape all her worry, escape the utter heartache of knowing the man she loved probably hated her now for a little while, if she'd just go to sleep.

But she remained where she was on the sofa, and even though she told herself she'd cry later, tears seeped from her eyes and ran down her cheeks faster and faster.

She felt as alone now as she had years ago when her father had suddenly died and she'd just realized she was pregnant. She'd find her strength tomorrow, and somehow or other she'd weather the storm that she feared was coming. Tomorrow she'd be strong for Andy, but tonight she had no more strength left. She just felt sad and anxious about what would happen next.

She was just about to head to her bedroom when she heard a soft knock on her door. Instantly her stomach clenched into a million knots. It could only be one person.

She opened the door to Jake. He looked tense and imposing and incredibly handsome dressed in a navy polo shirt and jeans. "Can I come in?" he asked.

Nodding, she opened the door wider to allow him entry. He took a seat on the sofa, his features unreadable. She closed the door and took a seat in the chair opposite him, her heart beating fast and furiously as she faced him.

"Needless to say, we need to talk," he said.

"I know," she replied.

"How are you feeling?" He frowned. "Your throat is really bruised."

She reached a hand up and touched her tender neck. "It's sore, and to be honest, I kind of feel like I was run over by a big truck this morning. But it will be fine." The last thing she wanted was any pity from him.

"Is Andy sleeping?"

"Yes."

"Did you tell him about me?" he asked.

"No. I thought that was a conversation we needed to have with him together," she replied.

Was he prolonging what he was here to discuss with her on purpose? She couldn't stand the tension any longer. "Jake, have you decided what you intend to do concerning Andy?"

"I have." His gaze held hers intently. "I want full custody of Andy."

Eva's world crashed down around her. She could hear nothing but the explosion of her heart. It was her worst nightmare come true. She would never be able to stop him. He had all the money, and she had none to fight him in a court of law.

He got up from the sofa and approached where she sat. "Eva, I also want full custody of you," he continued. "I want to marry you and live here with you and my son. I want to ranch with you here on your land. I want to make more babies with you and live the life we once dreamed about, but I don't know what you want, and I don't want you to choose me because of Andy. If you don't want me, then we'll work out a reasonable coparenting relationship."

She gazed up at him as she slowly digested his words. "Oh Jake, I want you. You've always been in my heart and soul. I want that love we pledged to each other in the hayloft. I love you, Jake."

He grabbed her up from the chair and pulled her into his arms. His lips captured hers in a kiss that spoke of breathtaking passion and enduring love.

When the kiss ended, she smiled at him. "We'll tell Andy when he gets home from school tomorrow. He's going to be so happy, Jake."

"I loved Andy when I didn't know he was mine, and I love him now as my son. I loved you years ago, and I never stopped loving you, Eva." His eyes glowed with his happiness. "Can I spend the night with you?"

"You can spend all your nights with me," she replied.

"Do I have to sleep on that lumpy, uncomfortable sofa?"

She laughed. "You never have to sleep on that sofa again."

He kissed her once again, and Eva felt as if her life was finally complete. She would continue to raise her son with Jake as a partner.

There was nothing and nobody who could stop them from building the life they had once dreamed of, and it was going to be a life filled with laughter and happiness and love.

Epilogue

"Andy, slow down," Eva yelled to her son, who was running ahead of them to the pond.

Running at his heels was Princess, a black schnauzer who not only slept in Andy's room each night but also went almost everywhere her son went.

Princess was the first addition to the family, but there was also another addition coming in four months. Eva was pregnant, and both Andy and Jake were over the moon about it.

David was still in jail, facing a multitude of charges, but that hadn't stopped Jake and Eva from moving on with their lives.

They had gotten married two months after the attack on Eva. It had been an intimate affair with only the preacher and Stephanie as a witness. They had exchanged vows in the hayloft, making real the teenage vows they had once spoken to each other.

Jake now grabbed her hand as they headed toward the pond for a family outing of fishing. They reached the dock, where Eva and Jake sat side by side and Andy settled in next to them with Princess next to him.

"Happy?" Jake asked.

"Happier than I could ever imagine," she replied. "What about you?"

"I'm living my very best dream," he replied. He gazed at her with the light in his eyes that warmed her from head to toe.

"I'm living my very best dream, too," Andy said. "I've got a dad and a dog. What more could I want?"

Eva laughed. "You'd better want a little sister, because it won't be long and you'll have one. And we need to pick out a name for her."

"I'll be the best big brother you ever saw," Andy said.

"There's no doubt in my mind that you'll be a great big brother to little Posie," Jake said.

Andy laughed. "We can't call her Posie," he protested.

Jake continued to throw out names, making Andy laugh over and over again. Eva's heart filled with such love it nearly brought her to tears.

Finally, she had the happiness she'd wanted with the man she had always loved. Their love had survived family betrayals and death threats. Their relationship was built on forgiveness and passion and a love that had endured through space and time.

As the laughter of their son and Jake rode the breeze, and with the stir of new life inside her, Eva knew her future was going to be wonderful.

* * * * *

*Don't miss other suspenseful titles
by Carla Cassidy:*

48 Hour Lockdown
Desperate Measures
Desperate Intentions
Desperate Strangers

Available from Harlequin Intrigue!